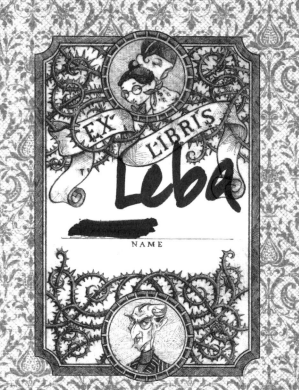

EX LIBRIS

Leba

NAME

THE ERSATZ ELEVATOR

A SERIES OF UNFORTUNATE EVENTS

A Series of Unfortunate Events

Book the Sixth

THE ERSATZ ELEVATOR

by

Lemony Snicket

Illustrated by
BRETT HELQUIST

EGMONT

First published in the USA 2001
by HarperCollins Children's Books
First published in Great Britain 2002
by Egmont Books Ltd
239 Kensington High Street, London W8 6SA

Published by arrangement with HarperCollins
Children's Books,
a division of HarperCollins Publishers, Inc.,
New York, New York, USA

ISBN 1 4052 0051 0

10 9 8 7 6 5 4 3 2 1

A CIP catalogue record for this title is available
from the British Library

Printed and bound in Italy

For Beatrice —
When we met, my life began.
Soon afterward, yours ended.

CHAPTER
One

The book you are holding in your two hands right now—assuming that you are, in fact, holding this book, and that you have only two hands—is one of two books in the world that will show you the difference between the word "nervous" and the word "anxious." The other book, of course, is the dictionary, and if I were you I would read that book instead.

Like this book, the dictionary shows you that the word "nervous" means "worried about something"—you might feel nervous, for instance, if you were served prune ice cream for dessert, because you would be worried that it would taste awful—whereas the word "anxious" means "troubled by disturbing suspense," which you might feel if you were served a live alligator for dessert, because you would be troubled by the disturbing suspense about whether you would eat your dessert or it would eat you. But unlike this book, the dictionary also discusses words that are far more pleasant to contemplate. The word "bubble" is in the dictionary, for instance, as is the word "peacock," the word "vacation," and the words "the" "author's" "execution" "has" "been" "canceled," which make up a sentence that is always pleasant to hear. So if you were to read the dictionary, rather than this book, you could skip the parts about "nervous" and "anxious" and read about things that wouldn't keep you up all night long, weeping and tearing out your hair.

But this book is not the dictionary, and if you were to skip the parts about "nervous" and "anxious" in this book, you would be skipping the most pleasant sections in the entire story. Nowhere in this book will you find the words "bubble," "peacock," "vacation," or, unfortunately for me, anything about an execution being canceled. Instead, I'm sorry to say, you will find the words "grief, "despair," and "woeful" as well as the phrases "dark passageway," "Count Olaf in disguise," and "the Baudelaire orphans were trapped," plus an assortment of miserable words and phrases that I cannot bring myself to write down. In short, reading a dictionary might make you feel nervous, because you would worry about finding it very boring, but reading this book will make you feel anxious, because you will be troubled by the disturbing suspense in which the Baudelaire orphans find themselves, and if I were you I would drop this book right out of your two or more hands and curl up with a dictionary instead, because all the miserable words I must use to describe these unfortunate events are about to reach your eyes.

"I imagine you must be nervous," Mr. Poe said. Mr. Poe was a banker who had been put in charge of the Baudelaire orphans following the death of their parents in a horrible fire. I am sorry to say that Mr. Poe had not done a very good job so far, and that the Baudelaires had learned that the only thing they could rely on with Mr. Poe was that he always had a cough. Sure enough, as soon as he finished his sentence, he took out his white handkerchief and coughed into it.

The flash of white cotton was practically the only thing the Baudelaire orphans could see. Violet, Klaus, and Sunny were standing with Mr. Poe in front of an enormous apartment building on Dark Avenue, a street in one of the fanciest districts in the city. Although Dark Avenue was just a few blocks away from where the Baudelaire mansion had been, the three children had never been in this neighborhood before, and they had assumed that the "dark" in Dark Avenue was simply a name and nothing more, the way a street named George Washington Boulevard does not necessarily indicate that George Washington lives there or the way Sixth

Street has not been divided into six equal parts.
But this afternoon the Baudelaires realized that
Dark Avenue was more than a name. It was an
appropriate description. Rather than street-
lamps, placed at regular intervals along the side-
walk were enormous trees the likes of which the
children had never seen before—and which
they could scarcely see now. High above a thick
and prickly trunk, the branches of the trees
drooped down like laundry hung out to dry,
spreading their wide, flat leaves out in every
direction, like a low, leafy ceiling over the
Baudelaires' heads. This ceiling blocked out all
the light from above, so even though it was the
middle of the afternoon, the street looked as
dark as evening—if a bit greener. It was hardly
a good way to make three orphans feel welcome
as they approached their new home.

"You have nothing to be nervous about,"
Mr. Poe said, putting his handkerchief back in
his pocket. "I realize some of your previous
guardians have caused a little trouble, but I

think Mr. and Mrs. Squalor will provide you with a proper home."

"We're not nervous," Violet said. "We're too anxious to be nervous."

"'Anxious' and 'nervous' mean the same thing," Mr. Poe said. "And what do you have to be anxious about, anyway?"

"Count Olaf, of course," Violet replied. Violet was fourteen, which made her the eldest Baudelaire child and the one who was most likely to speak up to adults. She was a superb inventor, and I am certain that if she had not been so anxious, she would have tied her hair up in a ribbon to keep it out of her eyes while she thought of an invention that could brighten up her surroundings.

"Count Olaf?" Mr. Poe said dismissively. "Don't worry about him. He'll never find you here."

The three children looked at one another and sighed. Count Olaf had been the first guardian Mr. Poe had found for the orphans, and he was a person as shady as Dark Avenue. He had one long eyebrow, a tattoo of an eye on his ankle, and two filthy hands that he hoped to use to snatch away the Baudelaire fortune that the orphans would inherit as soon as Violet came of age. The children had convinced Mr. Poe to remove them from Olaf's care, but since then the count had pursued them with a dogged determination, a phrase which here means "everywhere they went, thinking up treacherous schemes and wearing disguises to try to fool the three children."

"It's hard not to worry about Olaf," Klaus said, taking off his glasses to see if it was easier to look around the gloom without them, "because he has our compatriots in his clutches." Although Klaus, the middle Baudelaire, was only twelve, he had read so many books that he frequently used words like "compatriots," which is a fancy word for "friends." Klaus was referring to the Quagmire triplets, whom the Baudelaires had met while they were attending boarding school. Duncan Quagmire was a reporter, and was always writing down useful information in his notebook. Isadora Quagmire was a poet, and used her notebook to write poetry. The third triplet, Quigley, had died in a fire before the Baudelaire orphans had the opportunity to meet him, but the Baudelaires were certain that he would have been as good a friend as his siblings. Like the Baudelaires, the Quagmires were orphans, having lost their parents in the same fire that claimed their brother's life, and also like the Baudelaires, the Quagmires had been left an enormous fortune, in the form of the famous Quagmire sapphires, which were very rare and valuable jewels. But unlike the Baudelaires, they had not been able to escape Count Olaf's clutches. Just when the Quagmires had learned some terrible secret about Olaf, he had snatched them away, and since then the Baudelaires had been so worried that they had scarcely slept a wink. Whenever they closed their eyes, they saw only the long, black car that had whisked the Quagmires away, and they heard only the sound of their friends shrieking one fragment of the dreadful secret they had learned. "V.F.D.!" Duncan had screamed, just before the car raced away, and the Baudelaires tossed and turned, and worried for their friends, and wondered what in the world V.F.D. could stand for.

"You don't have to worry about the Quagmires, either," Mr. Poe said confidently. "At least, not for much longer. I don't know if you happened to read the Mulctuary Money Management newsletter, but I have some very good news about your friends."

"Gavu?" Sunny asked. Sunny was the youngest Baudelaire orphan, and the smallest, too. She was scarcely larger than a salami. This size was usual for her age, but she had four teeth that were larger and sharper than those of any other baby I have ever seen. Despite the maturity of her mouth, however, Sunny usually talked in a way most people found difficult to understand. By "Gavu," for instance, she meant something along the lines of "The Quagmires have been found and rescued?" and Violet was quick to translate so Mr. Poe would understand.

"Better than that," Mr. Poe said. "I have been promoted. I am now the bank's Vice President in Charge of Orphan Affairs. That means that I am in charge not only of your situation, but of the Quagmire situation as well. I promise you that I will concentrate a great deal of my energy on finding the Quagmires and returning them to safety, or my name isn't"—here Mr. Poe interrupted himself to cough once more into his handkerchief, and the Baudelaires waited patiently until he finished—"Poe. Now, as soon as I drop you off here I am taking a three-week helicopter ride to a mountain peak where the Quagmires may have been spotted. It will be very difficult to reach me during that time, as the helicopter has no phone, but I will call you as soon as I get back with your young pals. Now, can you see the number on this building?

It's hard for me to tell if we're at the right place."

"I think it says 667," Klaus said, squinting in the dim green light.

"Then we're here," Mr. Poe said. "Mr. and Mrs. Squalor live in the penthouse apartment of 667 Dark Avenue. I think the door is *here*."

"No, it's over here," said a high, scratchy voice out of the darkness. The Baudelaires jumped a little in surprise, and turned to see a man wearing a hat with a wide brim and a coat that was much too big for him. The coat sleeves hung over his hands, covering them completely, and the brim of his hat covered most of his face. He was so difficult to see that it was no wonder that the children hadn't spotted him earlier. "Most of our visitors find it hard to spot the door," the man said. "That's why they hired a doorman."

"Well, I'm glad they did," Mr. Poe said. "My name is Poe, and I have an appointment with Mr. and Mrs. Squalor to drop off their new children."

"Oh, yes," the doorman said. "They told me you were coming. Come on in."

The doorman opened the door of the building and showed them inside to a room that was as dark as the street. Instead of lights, there were only a few candles placed on the floor, and the children could scarcely tell whether it was a large room or a small room they were standing in.

"My, it's dark in here," Mr. Poe said. "Why don't you ask your employers to bring in a good strong halogen lamp?"

"We can't," the doorman replied. "Right now, dark is in."

"In what?" Violet asked.

"Just 'in,'" the doorman explained. "Around here, people decide whether something is in, which means it's stylish and appealing, or out, which means it's not. And it changes all the time. Why, just a couple of weeks ago, dark was out, and light was in, and you should have seen this neighborhood. You had to wear sunglasses all the time or you'd hurt your eyes."

"Dark is in, huh?" Mr. Poe said. "Wait until I tell my wife. In the meantime, could you show us where the elevator is? Mr. and Mrs. Squalor live in the penthouse apartment, and I don't want to walk all the way to the top floor."

"Well, I'm afraid you'll have to," the doorman said. "There's a pair of elevator doors right over there, but they won't be of any use to you."

"Is the elevator out of order?" Violet asked. "I'm very good with mechanical devices, and I'd be happy to take a look at it."

"That's a very kind and unusual offer," the doorman said. "But the elevator isn't out of order. It's just out. The neighborhood decided that elevators were out, so they had the elevator shut down. Stairs are in, though, so there's still a way to get to the penthouse. Let me show you."

The doorman led the way across the lobby, and the Baudelaire orphans peered up at a very long, curved staircase made of wood, with a metal banister that curved alongside. Every few steps, they could see, somebody had placed more candles, so the staircase looked like nothing more than curves of flickering lights, growing dimmer as the staircase went farther and farther up, until they could see nothing at all.

"I've never seen anything like this," Klaus said.

"It looks more like a cave than a staircase," Violet said.

"Pinse!" Sunny said, which meant something like "Or outer space!"

"It looks like a long walk to me," Mr. Poe said, frowning. He turned to the doorman. "How many floors up does this staircase go?"

The doorman's shoulders shrugged underneath his oversized coat. "I can't remember," he said. "I think it's forty-eight, but it might be eighty-four."

"I didn't know buildings could be that high," Klaus said.

"Well, whether it's forty-eight or eighty-four," Mr. Poe said, "I don't have time to walk you children all the way up. I'll miss my helicopter.

You'll have to go up by yourselves, and tell Mr. and Mrs. Squalor that I send my regards."

"We have to walk up by ourselves?" Violet said.

"Just be glad you don't have any of your things with you," Mr. Poe said. "Mrs. Squalor said there was no reason to bring any of your old clothing, and I think it's because she wanted to save you the effort of dragging suitcases up all those stairs."

"You're not going to come with us?" Klaus asked.

"I simply don't have the time to accompany you," Mr. Poe said, "and that is that."

The Baudelaires looked at one another. The children knew, as I'm sure you know, that there is usually no reason to be afraid of the dark, but even if you are not particularly afraid of something, you might not want to get near it, and the orphans were a bit nervous about climbing all the way up to the penthouse without an adult walking beside them.

"If you're afraid of the dark," Mr. Poe said, "I suppose I could delay my search for the Quagmires, and take you to your new guardians."

"No, no," Klaus said quickly. "We're not afraid of the dark, and finding the Quagmires is much more important."

"Obog," Sunny said doubtfully.

"Just try to crawl as long as you can," Violet said to her sister, "and then Klaus and I will take turns carrying you. Good-bye, Mr. Poe."

"Good-bye, children," Mr. Poe said. "If there's any problem, remember you can always contact me or any of my associates at Mulctuary Money Management—at least, as soon as I get off the helicopter."

"There's one good thing about this staircase," the doorman joked, starting to walk Mr. Poe back to the front door. "It's all uphill from here."

The Baudelaire orphans listened to the doorman's chuckles as he disappeared into the darkness, and they walked up the first few steps. As I'm sure you know, the expression "It's all uphill from here" has nothing to do with walk-ing up stairs—it merely means that things will get better in the future. The children had under-stood the joke, but they were too anxious to laugh. They were anxious about Count Olaf, who might find them any minute. They were anxious about the Quagmire triplets, whom they might never see again. And now, as they began to walk up the candlelit stairway, they were anxious about their new guardians. They tried to imag-ine what sort of people would live on such a dark street, in such a dark building, and at the top of either forty-eight or eighty-four flights of very dark stairs. They found it difficult to believe that things would get better in the future when they lived in such gloomy and poorly lit surroundings. Even though a long, upward climb awaited them, as the Baudelaire orphans started walking into the darkness, they were too anxious to be-lieve it was all uphill from here.

CHAPTER
Two

In order to get a better sense of exactly how the Baudelaire orphans felt as they began the grueling journey up the stairs to Mr. and Mrs. Squalor's penthouse apartment, you might find it useful to close your eyes as you read this chapter, because the light was so dim from the small candles on the ground that it felt as if their eyes were closed even when they were looking as hard as they could. At each curve in the staircase, there was a door that led to the apartment on each floor, and a pair of sliding elevator doors. From behind the sliding doors, the youngsters of course heard nothing, as the elevator had been shut down, but behind the doors to the apartments the children could hear the noises of people who lived in the building. When they reached the seventh floor, they heard two men laugh as somebody told a joke. When they reached the twelfth floor, they heard the splashing of water as somebody took a bath. When they reached the nineteenth floor, they heard a woman say "Let them eat cake" in a voice with a strange accent.

"I wonder what people will hear when they walk by the penthouse apartment," Violet wondered out loud, "when we are living there."

"I hope they hear me turning pages," Klaus said. "Maybe Mr. and Mrs. Squalor will have some interesting books to read."

"Or maybe people will hear me using a wrench," Violet said. "I hope the Squalors have some tools they'd let me use for my inventing."

"Crife!" Sunny said, crawling carefully past one of the candles on the ground.

Violet looked down at her and smiled. "I don't think that will be a problem, Sunny," she said. "You usually find something or other to bite. Be sure to speak up when you want us to start carrying you."

"I wish somebody could carry *me*," Klaus said, clutching the banister for support. "I'm getting tired."

"Me too," Violet admitted. "You would think, after Count Olaf made us run all those laps when he was disguised as a gym teacher, that these stairs wouldn't tire us out, but that's not the case. What floor are we on, anyway?"

"I don't know," Klaus said. "The doors aren't numbered, and I've lost count."

"Well, we won't miss the penthouse," Violet said. "It's on the top floor, so we'll just keep walking until the stairs stop."

"I wish you could invent a device that could take us up the stairs," Klaus said.

Violet smiled, although her siblings couldn't see it in the darkness. "That device was invented

a long time ago," she said. "It's called an elevator. But elevators are out, remember?"

Klaus smiled too. "And tired feet are in,"
he said.

"Remember that time," Violet said, "when
our parents attended the Sixteenth Annual Run-
a-Thon, and their feet were so tired when they
got home that Dad prepared dinner while sitting on the kitchen floor, instead of standing?"

"Of course I remember," Klaus said. "We
had only salad, because they couldn't stand up
and reach the stove."

"It would have been a perfect meal for Aunt
Josephine," Violet said, remembering one of the
Baudelaires' previous guardians. "She never
wanted to use the stove, because she thought it
might explode."

"Pomres," Sunny said sadly. She meant
something along the lines of "As it turned
out, the stove was the least of Aunt Josephine's
problems."

"That's true," Violet said quietly, as the

children heard someone sneeze from behind a door.

"I wonder what the Squalors will be like," Klaus said.

"Well, they must be wealthy to live on Dark Avenue," Violet said.

"Akrofil," Sunny said, which meant "And they're not afraid of heights, that's for sure."

Klaus smiled and looked down at his sister. "You sound tired, Sunny," he said. "Violet and I can take turns carrying you. We'll switch every three floors."

Violet nodded in agreement with Klaus's plan, and then said "Yes" out loud because she realized that her nod was invisible in the gloom. They continued up the staircase, and I'm sorry to say that the two older Baudelaires took many, many turns holding Sunny. If the Baudelaires had been going up a staircase of regular size, I would write the sentence "Up and up they went," but a more appropriate sentence would begin "Up and up and up and up" and would take either forty-eight or eighty-four pages to reach "they went," because the staircase was so unbelievably lengthy. Occasionally, they would pass the shadowy figure of someone else walking down the stairs, but the children were too tired to say even "Good afternoon"—and, later, "Good evening"—to these other residents of 667 Dark Avenue. The Baudelaires grew hungry. They grew achy. And they grew very tired of gazing at identical candles and steps and doors.

Just when they could stand it no longer, they reached another candle and step and door, and about five flights after that the stairs finally ended and deposited the tired children in a small room with one last candle sitting in the middle of the carpet. By the light of the candle, the Baudelaire orphans could see the door to their new home, and across the way, two pairs of sliding elevator doors with arrowed buttons alongside.

"Just think," Violet said, panting from her long walk up the stairs, "if elevators were in, we would have arrived at the Squalor penthouse in just a few minutes."

"Well, maybe they'll be back in soon," Klaus said. "I hope so. The other door must be to the Squalors' apartment. Let's knock."

They knocked on the door, and almost instantly it swung open to reveal a tall man wearing a suit with long, narrow stripes down it. Such a suit is called a pinstripe suit, and is usually worn by people who are either movie stars or gangsters.

"I thought I heard someone approaching the door," the man said, giving the children a smile that was so big they could see it even in the dim room. "Please come in. My name is Jerome Squalor, and I'm so happy that you've come to stay with us."

"I'm very pleased to meet you, Mr. Squalor," Violet said, still panting, as she and her siblings walked into an entryway almost as dim as the staircase. "I'm Violet Baudelaire, and this is my brother, Klaus, and my sister, Sunny."

"Goodness, you sound out of breath," Mr. Squalor said. "Luckily, I can think of two things to do about that. One is that you can stop calling me Mr. Squalor and start calling me Jerome. I'll call you three by your first names, too, and that way we'll all save breath. The second thing is that I'll make you a nice, cold martini. Come right this way."

"A martini?" Klaus asked. "Isn't that an alcoholic beverage?"

"Usually it is," Jerome agreed. "But right now, alcoholic martinis are out. Aqueous martinis are in. An aqueous martini is simply cold water served in a fancy glass with an olive in it, so it's perfectly legal for children as well as for adults."

"I've never had an aqueous martini," Violet said, "but I'll try one."

"Ah!" Jerome said. "You're adventurous! I like that in a person. Your mother was adventurous, too. You know, she and I were very good friends a ways back. We hiked up Mount

Fraught with some friends—gosh, it must have been twenty years ago. Mount Fraught was known for having dangerous animals on it, but your mother wasn't afraid. But then, swooping out of the sky—"

"Jerome, who was that at the door?" called a voice from the next room, and in walked a tall, slender woman, also dressed in a pinstripe suit. She had long fingernails that were so strongly polished that they shone even in the dim light.

"The Baudelaire children, of course," Jerome replied.

"But they're not coming today!" the woman cried.

"Of course they are," Jerome said. "I've been looking forward to it for days and days! You know," he said, turning from the woman to the Baudelaires, "I wanted to adopt you from the moment I heard about the fire. But, unfortunately, it was impossible."

"Orphans were out then," the woman explained. "Now they're in."

"My wife is always very attentive to what's in and what's out," Jerome said. "I don't care about it much, but Esmé feels differently. She was the one who insisted on having the elevator removed. Esmé, I was just about to make them some aqueous martinis. Would you like one?"

"Oh, yes!" Esmé cried. "Aqueous martinis are in!" She walked quickly over to the children and looked them over. "I'm Esmé Gigi Geniveve Squalor, the city's sixth most important financial advisor," she announced grandly. "Even though I am unbelievably wealthy, you may call me Esmé. I'll learn your names later. I'm very happy you're here, because orphans are in, and when all my friends hear that I have three real live orphans, they'll be sick with jealousy, won't they, Jerome?"

"I hope not," Jerome said, leading the children down a long, dim hallway to a huge, dim room that had various fancy couches, chairs, and tables. At the far end of the room was a series of windows, all with their shades drawn so that no light could get in. "I don't like to hear of anybody getting sick. Well, have a seat, children, and we'll tell you a little bit about your new home."

The Baudelaires sat down in three huge chairs, grateful for the opportunity to rest their feet. Jerome crossed to one of the tables, where a pitcher of water sat next to a bowl of olives and some fancy glasses, and quickly prepared the aqueous martinis. "Here you go," he said, handing Esmé and the children each a fancy glass. "Let's see. In case you ever get lost, remember that your new address is 667 Dark Avenue in the penthouse apartment."

"Oh, don't tell them silly things like that," Esmé said, waving her long-nailed hand in front of her face as if a moth were attacking it. "Children, here are some things you should know. Dark is in. Light is out. Stairs are in. Elevators are out. Pinstripe suits are in. Those horrible clothes you are wearing are out."

"What Esmé means," Jerome said quickly,

"is that we want you to feel as comfortable here as possible."

Violet took a sip of her aqueous martini. She was not surprised to find that it tasted like plain water, with a slight hint of olive. She didn't like it much, but it did quench her thirst from the long climb up the stairs. "That's very nice of you," she said.

"Mr. Poe told me about some of your previous guardians," Jerome said, shaking his head. "I feel awful that you've had such terrible experiences, and that we could have cared for you the entire time."

"It couldn't be helped," Esmé said. "When something is out, it's out, and orphans used to be out."

"I heard all about this Count Olaf person, too," Jerome said. "I told the doorman not to let anyone in the building who looked even vaguely like that despicable man, so you should be safe."

"That's a relief," Klaus said.

"That dreadful man is supposed to be up on some mountain, anyway," Esmé said. "Remember, Jerome? That unstylish banker said he was going away in a helicopter to go find those twins he kidnapped."

"Actually," Violet said, "they're triplets. The Quagmires are good friends of ours."

"My word!" Jerome said. "You must be worried sick!"

"Well, if they find them soon," Esmé said, "maybe we'll adopt them, too. Five orphans! I'll be the innest person in town!"

"We certainly have room for them," Jerome said. "This is a seventy-one-bedroom apartment, children, so you will have your pick of rooms. Klaus, Poe mentioned something about your being interested in inventing things, is that right?"

"My sister's the inventor," Klaus replied. "I'm more of a researcher myself."

"Well, then," Jerome said. "You can have the bedroom next to the library, and Violet can have the one that has a large wooden bench, perfect for keeping tools. Sunny can be in the room between you two. How does that sound?"

That sounded absolutely splendid, of course, but the Baudelaire orphans did not get an opportunity to say so, because a telephone rang just at that instant.

"I'll get it! I'll get it!" Esmé cried, and raced across the room to pick up the phone. "Squalor residence," she said, into the receiver, and then waited as the person spoke on the other end. "Yes, this is Mrs. Squalor. Yes. Yes. Yes? Oh, thank you, thank you, thank you!" She hung up the phone and turned to the children. "Guess what?" she asked. "I have some fantastic news on what we were talking about!"

"The Quagmires have been found?" Klaus asked hopefully.

"Who?" Esmé asked. "Oh, them. No, they haven't been found. Don't be silly. Jerome, children, listen to me—dark is out! Regular light is in!"

"Well, I'm not sure I'd call that fantastic news," Jerome said, "but it will be a relief to get some light around this place. Come on, Baudelaires, help me open the shades and you can get a look at our view. You can see quite a bit from so high up."

"I'll go turn on all the lamps in the penthouse," Esmé said breathlessly. "Quickly, before anybody sees that this apartment is still dark!"

Esmé dashed from the room, while Jerome gave the three siblings a little shrug and walked across the room to the windows. The Baudelaires followed him, and helped him open the heavy shades that were covering the windows. Instantly, sunlight streamed into the room, making them squint as their eyes adjusted to regular light. If the Baudelaires had looked around the room now that it was properly illuminated, they would have seen just how fancy all the furniture was. The couches had pillows embroidered with silver. The chairs were all painted with gold paint. And the tables were made from wood chopped away from some of the most expensive trees in the world. But the Baudelaire orphans were not looking around the room, as luxurious as it was. They were looking out of the window onto the city below.

"Spectacular view, don't you think?" Jerome asked them, and they nodded in agreement. It was as if they were looking out on a tiny, tiny city, with matchboxes instead of buildings and bookmarks instead of streets. They could see tiny colored shapes that looked like various insects but were really all the cars and carriages in town, driving along the bookmarks until they reached the matchboxes where the tiny dots of people lived and worked. The Baudelaires could see the neighborhood where they had lived with their parents, and the parts of town where their friends had lived, and in a faint blue strip far, far away, the beach where they had received the terrible news that had begun all their misfortune.

"I knew you'd like it," Jerome said. "It's

very expensive to live in a penthouse apartment, but I think it's worth it for a view like this. Look, those tiny round boxes over there are orange juice factories. That sort of purplish building next to the park is my favorite restaurant. Oh, and look straight down—they're already cutting down those awful trees that made our street so dark."

"Of course they're cutting them down," Esmé said, hurrying back into the room and blowing out a few candles that were sitting on the mantelpiece. "Regular light is in—as in as aqueous martinis, pinstripes, and orphans."

Violet, Klaus, and Sunny looked straight down, and saw that Jerome was right. Those strange trees that had blocked out the sunlight on Dark Avenue, looking no taller than paper clips from such a great height, were being chopped down by little gardener dots. Even though the trees had made the street seem so gloomy, it seemed a shame to tear them all down, leaving bare stumps that, from the penthouse window, looked like thumbtacks. The three siblings looked at one another, and then back down to Dark Avenue. Those trees were no longer in, so the gardeners were getting rid of them. The Baudelaires did not like to think of what would happen when orphans were no longer in, either.

If you were to take a plastic bag and place it inside a large bowl, and then, using a wooden spoon, stir the bag around and around the bowl, you could use the expression "a mixed bag" to describe what you had in front of you, but you would not be using the expression in the same way I am about to use it now. Although "a mixed bag" sometimes refers to a plastic bag that has been stirred in a bowl, more often it is used to describe a situation that has both good parts and bad parts. An afternoon at a movie theater, for instance, would be a mixed bag if your favorite movie were showing, but if you had to eat gravel instead of popcorn. A trip to the zoo would be a very mixed bag if the weather were beautiful, but all of the man- and woman-eating lions were running around loose. And, for the Baudelaire orphans, their first few days with the Squalors were one of the most mixed bags they had yet encountered, because the good parts were very good, but the bad parts were simply awful.

One of the good parts was that the Baude-laires were living once more in the city where they were born and raised. After the Baudelaire parents had died, and after their disastrous stay with Count Olaf, the three children had been sent to a number of remote locations to live, and they sorely missed the familiar surroundings of their hometown. Each morning, after Esmé left for work, Jerome would take the children to some of their favorite places in town. Violet was happy to see that her favorite exhibits at the Verne Invention Museum had not been changed, so she could take another look at the mechanical demonstrations that had inspired her to be an inventor when she was just two years old. Klaus was delighted to revisit the Akhmatova Bookstore, where his father used to take him as a special treat, to buy an atlas or a volume of the encyclopedia. And Sunny was interested in visiting the Pincus Hospital where she was born, although her memories of this place were a little fuzzy.

But in the afternoons, the three children would return to 667 Dark Avenue, and it was this part of the Baudelaires' situation that was not nearly as pleasant. For one thing, the penthouse was simply too big. Besides the seventy-one bedrooms, there were a number of living rooms, dining rooms, breakfast rooms, snack rooms, sitting rooms, standing rooms, ballrooms, bathrooms, kitchens, and an assortment of rooms that seemed to have no purpose at all. The penthouse was so enormous that the Baudelaire orphans often found themselves hopelessly lost inside it. Violet would leave her bedroom to go brush her teeth and not find her way back for an hour. Klaus would accidentally leave his glasses on a kitchen counter and waste the whole afternoon trying to find the right kitchen. And Sunny would find a very comfortable spot for sitting and biting things and be unable to find it the next day. It was often difficult to spend any time with Jerome, simply because it was very difficult to find him amid all the fancy rooms of their new home, and the Baudelaires scarcely saw Esmé at all. They knew she went off to work every day and returned in the evenings, but even at the times when she was in the apartment with them, the three children scarcely caught a glimpse of the city's sixth most important financial advisor. It was as if she had forgotten all about the new members of her family, or was simply more interested in lounging around the rooms in the apartment rather than spending time with the three siblings. But the Baudelaire orphans did not really mind that

Esmé was absent so often. They much preferred spending time with one another, or with Jerome, rather than participating in endless conversations about what was in and what was out.

Even when the Baudelaires stayed in their bedrooms, the three children did not have such a splendid time. As he had promised, Jerome had given Violet the bedroom with the large wooden bench, which was indeed perfect for keeping tools, but Violet could find no tools in the entire penthouse. She found it odd that such an enormous apartment would have not even a socket wrench or one measly pair of pliers, but Esmé haughtily explained, when Violet asked her one evening, that tools were out. Klaus did have the Squalor library next to his bedroom, and it was a large and comfortable room with hundreds of books on its shelves. But the middle Baudelaire was disappointed to find that every single book was merely a description of what had been in and out during various times in history. Klaus tried to interest himself in books of this type, but it was so dull to read a snooty book like *Boots Were In in 1812* or *Trout: In France They're Out* that Klaus found himself spending scarcely any time in the library at all. And poor Sunny fared no better, a phrase which here means "also became bored in her bedroom." Jerome had thoughtfully placed a number of toys in her room, but they were the sort of toys designed for softer-toothed babies— squishy stuffed animals, cushioned balls, and assorted colorful pillows, none of which were the least bit fun to bite.

But what really mixed the Baudelaire bag was not the overwhelming size of the Squalor apartment, or the disappointments of a tool bench without tools, a library without interesting books, or nonchewable items of amusement. What really troubled the three children was the thought that the Quagmire triplets were undoubtedly experiencing things that were much, much worse. With every passing day, their worry for their friends felt like a heavy load on the

Baudelaires' shoulders, and the load only seemed heavier, because the Squalors refused to be of any assistance.

"I'm very, very tired of discussing your little twin friends," Esmé said one day, as the Baudelaires and the Squalors sipped aqueous martinis one evening in a living room the children had never seen before. "I know you're worried about them, but it's boring to keep blabbing on about it."

"We didn't mean to bore you," Violet said, not adding that it is terribly rude to tell people that their troubles are boring.

"Of course you didn't," Jerome said, picking the olive out of his fancy glass and popping it into his mouth before turning to his wife. "The children are concerned, Esmé, which is perfectly understandable. I know Mr. Poe is doing all he can, but maybe we can put our heads together and come up with something else."

"I don't have time to put my head together," Esmé said. "The In Auction is coming up, and

I have to devote all of my energy to making sure it's a success."

"The In Auction?" Klaus asked.

"An auction," Jerome explained, "is a sort of sale. Everyone gets together in a large room, and an auctioneer shows off a bunch of things that are available for purchase. If you see something you like, you call out how much you'd be willing to pay for it. That's called a bid. Then somebody else might call out a bid, and somebody else, and whoever calls out the highest price wins the auction and buys the item in question. It's terribly exciting. Your mother used to love them! I remember one time—"

"You forgot the most important part," Esmé interrupted. "It's called the In Auction because we're selling only things that are in. I always organize it, and it's one of the most smashing events of the year!"

"Smashi?" Sunny asked.

"In this case," Klaus explained to his younger sister, "the word 'smashing' doesn't mean that things got smashed up. It just means 'fabulous.'"

"And it *is* fabulous," Esmé said, finishing her aqueous martini. "We hold the auction at Veblen Hall, and we auction off only the innest things we can find, and best of all, all the money goes to a good cause."

"Which good cause?" Violet asked.

Esmé clapped her long-nailed hands together with glee. "Me! Every last bit of money that people pay at the auction goes right to me! Isn't that smashing?"

"Actually, dear," Jerome said, "I was thinking that this year, perhaps we should give the money to another good cause. For instance, I was just reading about this family of seven. The mother and father lost their jobs, and now they're so poor that they can't even afford to live in a one-room apartment. We might send some of the auction money to people like them."

"Don't talk nonsense," Esmé said crossly. "If we give money to poor people, then they won't be poor anymore. Besides, this year we're going to make heaps of money. I had lunch with twelve millionaires this morning, and eleven of them said they were definitely going to attend the In Auction. The twelfth one has to go to a birthday party. Just think of the money I'll make, Jerome! Maybe we could move to a bigger apartment!"

"But we just moved in a few weeks ago," Jerome said. "I'd rather spend some money on putting the elevator back in use. It's very tiring to climb all the way up to the penthouse."

"There you go, talking nonsense again," Esmé said. "If I'm not listening to my orphans babble about their kidnapped friends, I'm listening to you talk about out things like elevators. Well, we have no more time for chitchat in any case. Gunther is stopping by tonight, and I want you, Jerome, to take the children out for dinner."

"Who is Gunther?" Jerome asked.

"Gunther is the auctioneer, of course,"

Esmé replied. "He's supposed to be the innest auctioneer in town, and he's going to help me organize the auction. He's coming over tonight to discuss the auction catalog, and we don't want to be disturbed. That's why I want you to go out to dinner, and give us a little privacy."

"But I was going to teach the children how to play chess tonight," Jerome said.

"No, no, no," Esmé said. "You're going out to dinner. It's all arranged. I made a reservation at Café Salmonella for seven o'clock. It's six o'clock now, so you should get moving. You want to allow plenty of time to walk down all those stairs. But before you leave, children, I have a present for each of you."

At this, the Baudelaire children were taken aback, a phrase which here means "surprised that someone who was so selfish had purchased gifts for them," but sure enough, Esmé reached behind the dark red sofa she was sitting on, and brought out three shopping bags that had the words "In Boutique" written on them in fancy, curly script. With an elegant gesture, Esmé handed a bag to each Baudelaire.

"I thought if I bought you something you really wanted," she said, "you might stop all this chatter about the Quagmires."

"What Esmé means," Jerome added hurriedly, "is that we want you to be happy here in our home, even when you're worried about your friends."

"That's not what I mean at all," Esmé said, "but never mind. Open the bags, kids."

The Baudelaires opened their presents, and I'm sorry to say that the shopping bags were mixed bags as well. There are many, many things that are difficult in this life, but one thing that isn't difficult at all is figuring out whether someone is excited or not when they open a present. If someone is excited, they will often put exclamation points at the ends of their sentences to indicate their excited tone of voice. If they say "Oh!" for instance, the exclamation point would indicate that the person is saying

"Oh!" in an excited way, rather than simply saying "Oh," with a comma after it, which would indicate that the present is somewhat disappointing.

"Oh," Violet said, as she opened her present.

"Oh," Klaus said, as he opened his.

"Oh," Sunny said, as she tore open her shopping bag with her teeth.

"Pinstripe suits! I knew you'd be excited!" Esmé said. "You must have been mortified the last few days, walking around the city without wearing any pinstripes! Pinstripes are in, and orphans are in, so just imagine how in you'll be when you orphans are wearing pinstripes! No wonder you're so excited!"

"They didn't sound excited when they opened the presents," Jerome said, "and I don't blame them. Esmé, I thought we said that we'd buy Violet a tool kit. She's very enthusiastic about inventing, and I thought we'd support that enthusiasm."

"But I'm enthusiastic about pinstripe suits,

too," Violet said, knowing that you should always say that you are delighted with a present even when you don't like it at all. "Thank you very much."

"And Klaus was supposed to get a good almanac," Jerome continued. "I told you about his interest in the International Date Line, and an almanac is the perfect book to learn all about that."

"But I'm *very* interested in pinstripes," said Klaus, who could lie as well as his sister, when the need arose. "I really appreciate this gift."

"And Sunny," Jerome said, "was going to be given a large square made of bronze. It would have been attractive, and easily bitable."

"Ayjim," Sunny said. She meant something along the lines of "I love my suit. Thank you very much," even though she didn't mean it one bit.

"I know we discussed buying those silly items," Esmé said, with a wave of her long-nailed hand, "but tools have been out for weeks, almanacs have been out for months, and I received a phone call this afternoon informing me that large bronze squares are not expected to be in for at least another year. What's in now is pinstripes, Jerome, and I don't appreciate your trying to teach my new children that they should ignore what's in and what's out. Don't you want what's best for the orphans?"

"Of course," Jerome sighed. "I hadn't thought of it that way, Esmé. Well, children, I do hope you like your gifts, even though they don't exactly match up with your interests. Why don't you go change into your new suits, and we'll wear them to dinner?"

"Oh, yes!" Esmé said. "Café Salmonella is one of the innest restaurants. In fact, I think they don't even let you eat there if you're not wearing pinstripes, so go change. But hurry up! Gunther is due to arrive any minute."

"We'll hurry," Klaus promised, "and thank you again for our gifts."

"You're very welcome," Jerome said with a smile, and the children smiled back at him,

walked out of the living room, down a long hallway, across a kitchen, through another living
room, past four bathrooms, and so on and so on
and so on, eventually finding their way to their
bedrooms. They stood together for a minute
outside the three bedroom doors, looking sadly
into their shopping bags.

"I don't know how we're going to wear these
things," Violet said.

"I don't either," Klaus said. "And it's all the
worse knowing that we almost got presents we
really want."

"Puictiw," Sunny agreed glumly.

"Listen to us," Violet said. "We sound hopelessly spoiled. We're living in an enormous
apartment. We each have our own room. The
doorman has promised to watch out for Count
Olaf, and at least one of our new guardians is an
interesting person. And yet we're standing here
complaining."

"You're right," Klaus said. "We should make
the best of things. Getting a lousy present isn't

really worth complaining over—not when our friends are in such terrible danger. We're really very lucky to be here at all."

"Chittol," Sunny said, which meant something like "That's true. We should stop complaining and go change into our new outfits."

The Baudelaires stood together for another moment and nodded resolutely, a phrase which here means "tried to make themselves stop feeling ungrateful and put on the suits." But even though they didn't want to seem spoiled, even though they knew their situation was not a terrible one at all, and even though they had less than an hour to change into the suits, find Jerome, and walk down all those hundreds and hundreds of stairs, the three children could not seem to move. They simply stood in front of their bedroom doors and stared into their bags from the In Boutique.

"Of course," Klaus said finally, "no matter how lucky we are, the fact remains that these pinstripe suits are entirely too big for us."

Klaus spoke the truth. It was a truth that might help you understand why the Baudelaires were so disappointed with what was in their bags. It was a truth that might help you understand why the Baudelaires were so reluctant to go into their rooms and change into their pinstripe suits. And it was a truth that became even more obvious when the Baudelaires finally went into their rooms, and opened their bags and put on the gifts that Esmé had given them.

It is often difficult to tell if a piece of clothing will fit you or not until you try it on, but the Baudelaire children could tell the instant they first looked into the shopping bags that these clothes dwarfed them by comparison. The expression "dwarfed by comparison" has nothing to do with dwarves, who are dull creatures in fairy tales who spend their time whistling and cleaning house. "Dwarfed by comparison" simply means that one thing seems small when compared to another thing. A mouse would be dwarfed by comparison with an ostrich, which is much bigger, and an ostrich would be dwarfed by comparison with the city of Paris. And the Baudelaires were dwarfed by comparison with the pinstripe suits. When Violet put the pants part of her suit on, the legs of the suit stretched much, much farther than the legs of her body, so it was as if she had two huge noodles instead of feet. When Klaus put the jacket part of his suit on, the sleeves fell far, far past his hands, so his arms looked as if they had shrunk up inside his body. And Sunny's suit dwarfed her so much by comparison that it was as if she had pulled the covers over her in bed instead of changing her clothes. When the Baudelaires stepped back out of their bedrooms and met up again in the hallway, they were so dwarfed by comparison that they scarcely recognized one another.

"You look like you're skiing," Klaus said, pointing at his older sister's pant legs. "Except your skis are made of cloth instead of titanium alloy."

"You look like you remembered to put on your jacket, but forgot to put on your arms," Violet replied with a grin.

"Mmphmm!" Sunny shrieked, and even her two siblings couldn't understand what she was saying from beneath all the pinstriped cloth.

"Goodness, Sunny," Violet said, "I thought you were a lump in the carpet. Here, we'd better just tie one of the sleeves of the suit around you. Maybe tomorrow we can find a pair of scissors, and—"

"Nnphnn!" Sunny interrupted.

"Oh, don't be silly, Sunny," Klaus said. "We've seen you in your underwear hundreds of times. One more time won't matter." But Klaus was wrong. He wasn't wrong about the under-wear—if you are a baby, your family will see you in your underwear many times, and there's no use being embarrassed about it—but he was wrong in thinking that by saying "Nnphnn!" Sunny had been complaining about getting undressed in front of her siblings. Sunny's oversized suit had muffled the word she was really saying, and it was a word that still haunts me in my dreams as I toss and turn each night, images of Beatrice and her legacy filling my weary, grieving brain no matter where in the world I travel and no matter what important evidence I discover.

It is necessary once more to use the expression "dwarfed in comparison," in order to refer to what happened after Sunny said that fatal word out loud. For even though Violet and Klaus could not hear what Sunny had said, they learned instantly what their sister had meant. For as Sunny uttered the word, a long shadow was cast over the Baudelaires, and they looked up to see what was blocking the light. And when they looked, they felt everything about their lives become dwarfed in comparison to how trapped they felt, because this word, I'm sorry to say, was "Olaf."

CHAPTER
Four

If you are ever forced to take a chemistry class, you will probably see, at the front of the classroom, a large chart divided into squares, with different numbers and letters in each of them. This chart is called the table of the elements, and scientists like to say that it contains all the substances that make up our world. Like everyone else, scientists are wrong from time to time, and it is easy to see that they are wrong about the table of the elements. Because although this table contains a great many elements, from the element oxygen, which is found in the air, to the element aluminum, which is found in cans of soda, the table of the elements does not contain one of the most powerful elements that make up our world, and that is the element of surprise. The element of surprise is not a gas, like oxygen, or a solid, like aluminum. The element of surprise is an unfair advantage, and it can be found in situations in which one person has sneaked up on another. The surprised person—or, in this sad case, the surprised persons—are too stunned to defend themselves, and the sneaky person has the advantage of the element of surprise.

"Hello, please," Count Olaf said in his raspy voice, and the Baudelaire orphans were too stunned to defend themselves. They did not scream. They did not run away from Olaf. They did not call out for their guardians to save them. They merely stood there, in their enormous pinstripe suits, and stared at the terrible man who had somehow found them once more.

As Olaf looked down at them with a nasty smile, enjoying the unfair advantage of the element of surprise, the children saw that he was in yet another of his nefarious disguises, a phrase which here means that he did not fool them one bit no matter what he was wearing. On Olaf's feet were a pair of shiny black boots with high tops that almost reached his knees—the sort of boots that someone might wear to ride a horse. Over one of Olaf's eyes was a monocle, which is an eyeglass for one eye, instead of two—the sort of eyewear that requires you to furrow your brow in order to keep it in place. And the rest of his body was covered in a pinstripe suit—the sort of suit that someone might wear in order to be in at the time when this story takes place. But the Baudelaires knew that Olaf didn't care about being in, any more than he had imperfect vision in one eye or was about to go horseback riding. The three children knew that Olaf was wearing boots to cover up the tattoo of an eye that he had on his left ankle. They knew he was wearing the monocle so that he could furrow his brow and make it difficult to see that he had only one long eyebrow over his shiny, shiny eyes. And they knew that he was wearing a pinstripe suit so that people would think he was a rich, in person who belonged on Dark Avenue, instead of a greedy, treacherous villain who belonged in a heavily guarded prison.

"You must be children, please," he continued, using the word "please" incorrectly for the second time. "The name of mine is Gunther. Please excuse the talking of me. Please, I am not fluent in the English language, please."

"How . . ." Violet said, and then stopped. She was was still stunned, and it was difficult to finish the sentence "How did you find us so quickly, and how did you get past the doorman, who promised to keep you away from us?" while under the element of surprise.

"Where . . ." Klaus said, and then stopped. He was as stunned as his sister, and he found it impossible to finish the sentence "Where have you put the Quagmire triplets?" while under the element of surprise.

"Bik . . ." Sunny said, and stopped. The element of surprise weighed down on the youngest Baudelaire as heavily as it did on Violet and Klaus, and Sunny could not find the words to finish the sentence "Bikayado?" which meant something like "What new evil plan have you cooked up to steal our fortune?"

"I see you are not fluent in the English language either, please," Count Olaf said, continuing to fake a different way of talking. "Where is the mother and father?"

"We're not the mother and father," Esmé said, and the Baudelaires felt another element of surprise as the Squalors walked into the hallway from another door. "We're the legal guardians. These children are orphans, Gunther."

"Ah!" From behind his monocle, Count Olaf's eyes grew even shinier, as they often did when he was looking down on the helpless Baudelaires. The children felt as if his eyes were a pair of lit matches, about to burn them to a crisp. "Orphans in!" he said.

"I know orphans are in," Esmé said, ignoring Olaf's improper grammar. "In fact, they're so in they ought to be auctioned off next week at the big event!"

"Esmé!" Jerome said. "I'm shocked! We're not going to auction off these children."

"Of course we're not," Esmé said. "It's against the law to auction off children. Oh, well. Come along, Gunther. I'll give you a full tour of our apartment. Jerome, take the children to Café Salmonella."

"But we haven't even introduced them," Jerome said. "Violet, Klaus, Sunny—meet Gunther, the auctioneer we were talking about earlier. Gunther, meet the newest members of our family."

"I am happy to meet you, please," Olaf said, reaching out one of his scraggly hands.

"We've met before," Violet said, happy to see that the element of surprise was fading away and that she was finding the courage to speak up. "*Many* times before. Jerome and Esmé, this man is an impostor. He's not Gunther and he's not an auctioneer. This is Count Olaf."

"I am not understanding, please, what the orphan is saying," Olaf said. "Please, I am not fluent in the English language, please."

"Yes you are," said Klaus, who also found himself feeling more courageous than surprised. "You speak English perfectly."

"Why, Klaus, I'm surprised at you!" Jerome said. "A well-read person such as yourself should know he made a few grammatical errors."

"Waran!" Sunny shrieked.

"My sister is right," Violet said. "His improper English is just part of his disguise. If you make him take off his boots, you'll see his tattoo, and if you make him take off his monocle, his brow will unfurrow, and—"

"Gunther is one of the innest auctioneers in

the world," Esmé said impatiently. "He told me
so himself. I'm not going to make him get undressed just to make you feel better. Now shake
Gunther's hand, and go off to dinner and we'll
say no more about it."

"He's not Gunther, I tell you!" Klaus cried.
"He's Count Olaf."

"I am not knowing what you are saying,
please," Count Olaf said, shrugging his scrawny
shoulders.

"Esmé," Jerome said hesitantly. "How can
we be sure this man is really who he says he is?
The children do seem quite alarmed. Perhaps
we should—"

"Perhaps we should listen to me," Esmé
said, pointing one long-nailed finger at herself.
"I am Esmé Gigi Geniveve Squalor, the city's
sixth most important financial advisor. I live on
Dark Avenue, and I am unbelievably wealthy."

"I know that, dear," Jerome said. "I live with
you."

"Well, if you want to continue to live with

me, you will call this man by his proper name, and this goes for you three children as well. I go to the trouble of buying you some smashing pinstripe suits, and you start accusing people of being in disguise!"

"It is O.K., please," Count Olaf said. "The children are confused."

"We're not confused, Olaf," Violet said.

Esmé turned to Violet and gave her an angry glare. "You and your siblings will call this man Gunther," she ordered, "or you will make me very, very sorry I took you into my glamorous home."

Violet looked at Klaus, and then at Sunny, and quickly made a decision. Arguing with somebody is never pleasant, but sometimes it is useful and necessary to do so. Just the other day, for example, it was useful and necessary for me to have an unpleasant argument with a medical student, because if he hadn't let me borrow his speedboat I would now be chained inside a very small, waterproof room, instead of sitting in a typewriter factory typing out this woeful tale. But Violet realized that it was neither useful nor necessary to argue with Esmé, because her guardian had clearly made up her mind about Gunther. It would be more useful and necessary to leave the penthouse and try to figure out what to do about the reappearance of this dreadful villain, instead of standing there and bickering over what name to call him, so Violet took a deep breath and smiled up at the man who had brought so much trouble into the Baudelaire lives.

"I'm sorry, Gunther," she said, almost choking on her false apology.

"But—" Klaus started to argue, but Violet gave him a look that meant the Baudelaires would discuss the matter later, when there weren't any adults around. "That's right," he said quickly, understanding his sister's glance at once. "We thought you were someone else, sir."

Gunther reached up to his face and adjusted his monocle. "O.K., please," he said.

"It's so much nicer when no one is arguing," Jerome said. "Come on, children, let's go to dinner. Gunther and Esmé have to plan the auction, and they need the apartment to themselves."

"Let me just take a minute to roll up my sleeves," Klaus replied. "Our suits are a little big."

"First you complain that Gunther is an impostor, then you complain about your suits," Esmé said, rolling her eyes. "I guess it goes to show you that orphans can be in and rude at the same time. Come on, Gunther, let me show you the rest of my glorious apartment."

"See you later, please," Gunther said to the children, his eyes shining brightly, and gave them a little wave as he followed Esmé down the hallway. Jerome waved back, but as soon as Gunther was around the corner, he leaned in close to the children.

"That was very nice of you to stop arguing with Esmé," he said. "I could tell that you weren't completely convinced you had made a mistake about Gunther. But don't worry. There is something we can do to set your minds at ease."

The Baudelaires looked at one another and smiled in relief. "Oh, thank you, Jerome," Violet said. "What did you have in mind?"

Jerome smiled, and knelt down to help Violet roll up the legs of her suit. "I wonder if you can guess," he said.

"We could make Gunther take off his boots," she said, "and we could see if he had Olaf's tattoo."

"Or we could make him remove his monocle and unfurrow his brow," Klaus said, as he rolled up his sleeves, "and we could get a better look at his eyebrow situation."

"Resyca!" Sunny said, which meant something like "Or you could simply ask him to leave the penthouse, and never return!"

"Well, I don't know what 'Resyca!' means," Jerome said, "but we're not going to do those other things. Gunther is a guest, and we don't want to be rude to him."

The Baudelaires actually did want to be rude to him, but they knew it was rude to say so. "Then what will set our minds at ease?" Violet asked.

"Instead of climbing down all those stairs," Jerome said, "we can slide down the banister! It's great fun, and whenever I do it, it takes my mind off my troubles, no matter what they are. Follow me!"

Sliding down a banister, of course, was not going to make the Baudelaires feel any better about an evil person lurking around their home, but before any of them could say so, Jerome was already leading the way out of the penthouse. "Come on, Baudelaires!" he called, and the children followed him as he walked quickly down the hallway, through four sitting rooms, across a kitchen, past nine bedrooms, and finally out of the apartment. He led the youngsters past the two pairs of elevator doors to the top of the staircase, and sat on the banister with a wide grin.

"I'll go first," he said, "so you'll see how it's done. Be careful on the curvy parts, and if you're going too fast you can slow yourself down by scraping your shoes along the wall. Don't be scared!"

Jerome gave himself a push, and in a second he had slid out of view, his laughter echoing off the stairwell as he raced down toward the lobby. The children looked down the stairway and felt their hearts sink with fear. It was not the fear of sliding down the banister. The Baudelaires had slid down plenty of banisters, and although they had never slid down one that was either forty-eight or eighty-four stories high, they were not scared to try, particularly now that regular light was in so they could see where they were going. But they were afraid nonetheless. They were afraid that Gunther had a clever and nasty scheme to get his hands on the Baudelaire fortune, and that they didn't have the faintest idea of what it was. They were afraid that something dreadful had happened to the Quagmire triplets, because Gunther seemed to have time to find the Baudelaires here in their new home. And they were afraid that the Squalors would not be of any assistance in keeping the three children safe from Gunther's crooked clutches.

Jerome's laughter grew fainter and fainter as he slid farther and farther away, and as they stood together without a word and looked down the stairway, which curved and curved and curved as far as their eyes could see, the Baudelaire orphans were afraid that it was all downhill from here.

Café Salmonella was located in the Fish District, which was a part of the city that looked, sounded, smelled, and—if you were to kneel down and lick its streets—probably tasted like fish. The Fish District smelled like fish because it was located near the docks of the city, where fishermen sold the fish they had caught each morning. It sounded like fish because the pavement was always wet from the sea breeze, and the feet of passersby made bubbly, splashy sounds that resembled the noises made by sea creatures. And it looked like fish because all of the buildings in the Fish District were made of shiny, silvery scales, instead of bricks or wooden planks. When the Baudelaire orphans arrived at the Fish District and followed Jerome to Café Salmonella, they had to look up at the evening sky to remind themselves that they were not underwater.

Café Salmonella was not just a restaurant, but a theme restaurant, which simply means a restaurant with food and decorations that follow a certain idea. The theme for Café Salmonella— and you can probably guess this from its name— was salmon. There were pictures of salmon on the walls, and drawings of salmon on the menu, and the waiters and waitresses were dressed up in salmon costumes, which made it difficult for them to carry plates and trays. The tables were decorated with vases full of salmon, instead of flowers, and of course all of the food that Café

Salmonella served had something to do with salmon. There is nothing particularly wrong with salmon, of course, but like caramel candy, strawberry yogurt, and liquid carpet cleaner, if you eat too much of it you are not going to enjoy your meal. And so it was that evening with the Baudelaire orphans. Their costumed waiter first brought bowls of creamy salmon soup to the table, and then some chilled salmon salad and then some broiled salmon served with salmon ravioli in a salmon butter sauce for a main course, and by the time the waiter brought over salmon pie with a scoop of salmon ice cream on top the children never wanted to have another bite of salmon again. But even if the meal had featured a variety of foods, all cooked deliciously and brought by a waiter dressed in a simple, comfortable outfit, the Baudelaires would not have enjoyed their dinner, because the thought of Gunther spending the evening alone with their guardian made them lose their appetite far more than too much pink, flavorful fish, and

Jerome was simply not willing to discuss the matter any further.

"I am simply not willing to discuss the matter any further," Jerome said, taking a sip from his water glass, which had chunks of frozen salmon floating in it instead of ice cubes. "And frankly, Baudelaires, I think you should be a little ashamed of your suspicions. Do you know what the word 'xenophobe' means?"

Violet and Sunny shook their heads, and looked over at their brother, who was trying to remember if he had come across the word in one of his books. "When a word ends in '-phobe,'" Klaus said, wiping his mouth with a salmon-shaped napkin, "it usually means somebody who is afraid of something. Does 'xeno' mean 'Olaf'?"

"No," Jerome said. "It means 'stranger,' or 'foreigner.' A xenophobe is somebody who is afraid of people just because they come from a different country, which is a silly reason for fear. I would have thought that you three would be far too sensible to be xenophobes. After all,

Violet, Galileo came from a country in Europe, and he invented the telescope. Would you be afraid of him?"

"No," Violet said. "I'd be honored to meet him. But—"

"And Klaus," Jerome continued, "surely you've heard of the writer Junichiro Tanizaki, who came from a country in Asia. Would you be afraid of him?"

"Of course not," Klaus said. "But—"

"And Sunny," Jerome continued. "The sharp-toothed mountain lion can be found in a number of countries in North America. Would you be afraid if you met a mountain lion?"

"Netesh," Sunny said, which meant something like "Of course I would! Mountain lions are wild animals," but Jerome continued talking as if he hadn't heard a word she said.

"I don't mean to scold you," he said. "I know you've had a very difficult time since your parents' death, and Esmé and I want to do all we can to provide a good, safe home for you.

I don't think Count Olaf would dare come to our fancy neighborhood, but in case he does, the doorman will spot him and alert the authorities immediately."

"But the doorman didn't spot him," Violet insisted. "He was in disguise."

"And Olaf would dare to go anywhere to find us," Klaus added. "It doesn't matter how fancy the neighborhood is."

Jerome looked uncomfortably at the children. "Please don't argue with me," he said. "I can't stand arguing."

"But sometimes it's useful and necessary to argue," Violet said.

"I can't think of a single argument that would be useful or necessary," Jerome said. "For instance, Esmé made reservations for us here at Café Salmonella, and I can't stand the taste of salmon. I could have argued with her about that, of course, but why would it be useful or necessary?"

"Well, you could have had a dinner that you enjoyed," Klaus said.

Jerome shook his head. "Someday, when you're older, you'll understand," he said. "In the meantime, do you remember which salmon is our waiter? It's close to your bedtime, and I'd like to pay the bill and take you home."

The Baudelaire orphans looked at one another in frustration and sadness. They were frustrated from trying to convince Jerome of Gunther's true identity, and they were sad because they knew it was no use to keep on trying. They scarcely said another word as Jerome ushered them out of Café Salmonella and into a taxicab that drove them out of the Fish District to 667 Dark Avenue. On the way, the taxicab passed the beach where the Baudelaires had first heard the terrible news about the fire, a time that seemed in the very, very distant past, even though it had not been all that long ago, and as the children stared out the window at the ocean waves rippling along the dark, dark beach, they missed their parents more than ever. If the Baudelaire parents had been alive, they would have listened to their children. They would have believed them when they told them who Gunther really was. But what made the Baudelaires saddest of all was the fact that if the Baudelaire parents had been alive, the three siblings would not even know who Count Olaf was, let alone be the objects of his treacherous and greedy plans. Violet, Klaus, and Sunny sat in the taxi and stared mournfully out the window, and they wished with all their might that they could return to the time when their lives were happy and carefree.

"You're back already?" the doorman asked, as he opened the door of the taxi with a hand still hidden in the sleeve of his coat. "Mrs. Squalor said that you were not supposed to return until your guest left the penthouse, and he hasn't come down yet."

Jerome looked at his watch and frowned. "It's quite late," he said. "The children should be in bed soon. I'm sure if we're very quiet, we won't disturb them."

"I had very strict instructions," the doorman said. "Nobody is supposed to enter the penthouse apartment until the guest leaves the building, which he definitely has not done."

"I don't want to argue with you," Jerome said. "But perhaps he's on his way down now. It takes a long time to get down all those stairs, unless you're sliding down the banister. So it might be O.K. for us to go up."

"I never thought of that," the doorman said, scratching his chin with his sleeve. "All right, I guess you can go up. Maybe you'll run into him on the stairs."

The Baudelaire children looked at one another. They weren't sure which made them more nervous—the idea that Gunther had spent so much time in the Squalor penthouse, or the idea that they might meet him as he came down the stairs. "Maybe we *should* wait for Gunther to leave," Violet said. "We don't want the doorman to get in trouble."

"No, no," Jerome decided. "We'd best start the climb or we'll be too tired to reach the top. Sunny, be sure to let me know when you want me to carry you."

They walked into the lobby of the building and were surprised to see that it had been completely redecorated while they were at dinner. All the walls were painted blue, and the floor was covered in sand, with a few seashells scattered in the corners.

"Ocean decorating is in," the doorman explained. "I just got the phone call today. By tomorrow, the lobby will be filled with underwater scenery."

"I wish we'd known about this earlier," Jerome said. "We would have brought something back from the Fish District."

"Oh, I wish you had," the doorman said.

"Everybody wants ocean decorations now, and they're getting hard to find."

"There are sure to be some ocean decorations for sale at the In Auction," Jerome said, as he and the Baudelaires reached the beginning of the stairway. "Maybe you should stop by and purchase something for the lobby."

"Maybe I will," the doorman said, smiling oddly at the children. "Maybe I will. Have a good evening, folks."

The Baudelaires said good night to the doorman, and began the long climb up the stairs. Up and up and up they climbed, and they passed a number of people who were on their way down, but although all of them were in pinstripe suits, none of them were Gunther. As the children climbed higher and higher, the people going down the stairs looked more and more tired, and each time the Baudelaires passed an apartment door, they heard the sounds of people getting ready for bed. On the seventeenth floor, they heard somebody ask their mother where the bubble bath was. On the thirty-eighth floor, they heard the sounds of somebody brushing their teeth. And on a floor very high up—the children had lost count again, but it must have been quite high, because Jerome was carrying Sunny—they heard someone with a deep, deep voice, reading a children's story out loud. All these sounds made them sleepier and sleepier, and by the time they reached the top floor the Baudelaire orphans were so tired it felt as if they were sleepwalking, or, in Sunny's case, being sleep-carried. They were so tired that they almost dozed off, leaning against the two sets of sliding elevator doors, as Jerome unlocked the front door. And they were so tired that it seemed as if Gunther's appearance had been a dream, because when they asked about him, Esmé replied that he had left a long time ago.

"Gunther left?" Violet asked. "But the door-man said that he was still here."

"Oh, no," Esmé said. "He dropped off a

catalog of all the items for the In Auction. It's in the library if you want to look at it. We went over some auctioneering details, and then he went home."

"But that can't be," Jerome said.

"Of course it can be," Esmé replied. "He walked right out the front door."

The Baudelaires looked at one another in confusion and suspicion. How had Gunther managed to leave the penthouse without being spotted? "Did he take an elevator when he left?" Klaus said.

Esmé's eyes widened, and she opened and shut her mouth several times without saying anything, as if she were experiencing the element of surprise. "No," she said finally. "The elevator's been shut down. You know that."

"But the doorman said he was still here," Violet said again. "And we didn't see him when we walked up the stairs."

"Well, then the doorman was wrong," Esmé

said. "But let's not have any more of this somniferous conversation. Jerome, put them right to bed."

The Baudelaires looked at one another. They didn't think the conversation was at all somniferous, a fancy word for something that is so boring it puts you to sleep. Despite their exhausting climb, the children did not feel the least bit tired when they were talking about Gunther's whereabouts. The idea that he had managed to disappear as mysteriously as he had appeared made them too anxious to be sleepy. But the three siblings knew that they would not be able to convince the Squalors to discuss it any futher, any more than they had been able to convince them that Gunther was Count Olaf instead of an in auctioneer, so they said good night to Esmé and followed Jerome across three ballrooms, past a breakfast room, through two sitting rooms, and eventually to their own bedrooms.

"Good night, children," Jerome said, and

smiled. "The three of you will probably sleep like logs, after all that climbing. I don't mean that you resemble parts of trees, of course. I just mean that once you get into bed, I bet you'll fall right asleep and won't move any more than a log does."

"We know what you meant, Jerome," Klaus replied, "and I hope you're right. Good night."

Jerome smiled at the children, and the children smiled back, and then looked at each other once more before walking into their bedrooms and shutting the doors behind them. The children knew that they would not sleep like logs, unless there were certain logs that tossed and turned all night wondering things. The siblings wondered where Gunther was hiding, and how he had managed to find them, and what terrible treachery he was dreaming up. They wondered where the Quagmire triplets were, since Gunther had time to prey on the Baudelaires. And they wondered what V.F.D. could mean, and if it would help them with Gunther if they knew.

The Baudelaires tossed and turned, and wondered about all these things, and as it grew later and later they felt less and less like logs and more and more like children in a sinister and mysterious plot, spending one of the least somniferous nights of their young lives.

CHAPTER

Six

Morning is one of the best times for thinking. When one has just woken up, but hasn't yet gotten out of bed, it is a perfect time to look up at the ceiling, consider one's life, and wonder what the future will hold. The morning I am writing this chapter, I am wondering if the future will hold something that will enable me to saw through these handcuffs and crawl out of the double-locked window, but in the case of the Baudelaire orphans, when the morning sun shone through the eight hundred and forty-nine windows in the Squalor penthouse, they were wondering if the future would hold knowledge of the trouble they felt closing in around them.

Violet watched the first few rays of sunlight brighten her sturdy, tool-free workbench, and tried to imagine what sort of evil plan Gunther had cooked up. Klaus watched the dawn's rays make shifting shapes on the wall that separated his room from the Squalor library, and racked his brain for a way Gunther could have vanished into thin air. And Sunny watched the emerging sun illuminate all of the unbiteable baby toys, and tried to figure out if they had time to discuss the matter together before the Squalors came to wake them up.

This last thing was fairly easy to figure out. The littlest Baudelaire crawled out her bedroom door, fetched her brother, and opened Violet's door to find her out of bed and sitting at her wooden workbench with her hair tied up in a ribbon to keep it out of her eyes.

"Tageb," Sunny said.

"Good morning," Violet replied. "I thought it might help me think if I tied my hair up, and sat at my workbench, as if I were inventing something. But I haven't figured out a thing."

"It's terrible enough that Olaf has shown up again," Klaus said, "and that we have to call him Gunther. But we don't have the faintest clue what he's planning."

"Well, he wants to get his hands on our fortune, that's for sure," Violet said.

"Klofy," Sunny said, which meant "Of course. But how?"

"Maybe it has something to do with the In Auction," Klaus guessed. "Why would he disguise himself as an auctioneer if it weren't part of his plan?"

Sunny yawned, and Violet reached down and lifted up her sister so she could sit on her lap. "Do you think he's going to try to auction us off?" Violet asked, as Sunny leaned forward to nibble on the workbench in thought. "He could get one of those terrible assistants of his to bid higher and higher for us until he won, and then we'd be in his clutches, just like the poor Quagmires."

"But Esmé said it's against the law to auction off children," Klaus pointed out.

Sunny stopped chewing on the workbench and looked at her siblings. "Nolano?" she asked, which meant something like "Do you think the Squalors are working together with Gunther?"

"I don't think so," Violet said. "They've been very kind to us—well, Jerome has, at least—and anyway, they don't need the Baudelaire fortune. They have so much money already."

"But not much common sense," Klaus said unhappily. "Gunther fooled them completely, and all it took were some black boots, a pinstripe suit, and a monocle."

"Plus, he fooled them into thinking that he had left," Violet said, "but the doorman was certain that he hadn't."

"Gunther's got me fooled, too," Klaus said. "How could he have left without the doorman noticing?"

"I don't know," Violet said miserably. "The whole thing is like a jigsaw puzzle, but there are too many missing pieces to solve it."

"Did I hear someone say 'jigsaw puzzles'?" Jerome asked. "If you're looking for some jigsaw puzzles, I think there are a few in the cabinet in one of the sitting rooms, or maybe in one of the living rooms, I can't remember which."

The Baudelaires looked up and saw their guardian standing in the doorway of Violet's bedroom with a smile on his face and a silver tray in his hands.

"Good morning, Jerome," Klaus said. "And thank you, but we're not looking for a jigsaw puzzle. Violet was just using an expression. We're trying to figure something out."

"Well, you'll never figure anything out on an empty stomach," Jerome replied. "I have some breakfast here for you: three poached eggs and some nice whole wheat toast."

"Thank you," Violet said. "It's very nice of you to fix us breakfast."

"You're very welcome," Jerome replied. "Esmé has an important meeting with the King of Arizona today, so we have the whole day to ourselves. I thought we could walk across town to the Clothing District, and take your pinstripe suits to a good tailor. There's no use having those suits if they don't fit you properly."

"Knilliu!" Sunny shrieked, which meant "That's very considerate of you."

"I don't know what 'Knilliu!' means," Esmé said, walking into the bedroom, "and I don't care, but neither will you when you hear the fantastic news I just received on the phone! Aqueous martinis are out, and parsley soda is in!"

"Parsley soda?" Jerome said, frowning. "That sounds terrible. I think I'll stick to aqueous martinis."

"You're not listening," Esmé said. "Parsley soda is in now. You'll have to go out right now and buy a few crates of it."

"But I was going to take the children's suits to the tailor today," Jerome said.

"Then you'll have to change your plans," Esmé said impatiently. "The children already have clothing, but we don't have any parsley soda."

"Well, I don't want to argue," Jerome said.

"Then don't argue," Esmé replied. "And don't take the children with you, either. The Beverage District is no place for young people. Well, we'd better go, Jerome. I don't want to be late for His Arizona Highness."

"But don't you want to spend some time with the Baudelaires before the work day begins?" Jerome asked.

"Not particularly," Esmé said, and looked briefly at her watch. "I'll just say good morning to them. Good morning. Well, let's go, Jerome."

Jerome opened his mouth as if he had something else to say, but Esmé was already marching out of the bedroom, so he just shrugged. "Have a good day," he said to the children. "There's food in all of our kitchens, so you can make yourselves lunch. I'm sorry that our plans didn't work out after all."

"Hurry up!" Esmé called, from down the

hallway, and Jerome ran out of the room. The children heard their guardians' footsteps grow fainter and fainter as they made their way to the front door.

"Well," Klaus said, when they couldn't hear them anymore, "what shall we do today?"

"Vinfrey," Sunny said.

"Sunny's right," Violet said. "We'd better spend the day figuring out what Gunther's up to."

"How can we know what he's up to," Klaus said, "when we don't even know where he is?"

"Well, we'd better find out," Violet said. "He already had the unfair advantage of the element of surprise, and we don't want him to have the unfair advantage of a good hiding place."

"This penthouse has lots of good hiding places," Klaus said. "There are so many rooms."

"Koundix," Sunny said, which meant something like "But he can't be in the penthouse. Esmé saw him leave."

"Well, maybe he sneaked back in," Violet

said, "and is lurking around right now."

The Baudelaires looked at one another, and then at Violet's doorway, half expecting to see Gunther standing there looking at them with his shiny, shiny eyes.

"If he was lurking around here," Klaus said, "wouldn't he have grabbed us the instant the Squalors went out?"

"Maybe," Violet said. "If that was his plan."

The Baudelaires looked at the empty doorway again.

"I'm scared," Klaus said.

"Ecrif!" Sunny agreed.

"I'm scared, too," Violet admitted, "but if he's here in the penthouse, we'd better find out. We'll have to search the entire place and see if we find him."

"I don't want to find him," Klaus said. "Let's run downstairs and call Mr. Poe instead."

"Mr. Poe is in a helicopter, looking for the Quagmire triplets," Violet said. "By the time he returns it may be too late. We have to figure out what Gunther is up to—not only for our sake, but for the sake of Isadora and Duncan."

At the mention of the Quagmire triplets, all three Baudelaires felt a stiffening of their resolve, a phrase which here means "realized that they had to search the penthouse for Gunther, even though it was a scary thing to do." The children remembered how hard Duncan and Isadora had worked to save them from Olaf's clutches back at Prufrock Preparatory School, doing absolutely everything they could to help the Baudelaires escape Olaf's evil plan. The Quagmires had sneaked out in the middle of the night and put themselves in grave danger. The Quagmires had put on disguises, risking their lives in order to try to fool Olaf. And the Quagmires had done a lot of researching, finding out the secret of V.F.D.—although they had been snatched away before they could reveal the secret to the Baudelaires. Violet, Klaus, and Sunny thought about the two brave and loyal triplets, and knew they had to be just as brave and loyal, now that they had an opportunity to save their friends.

"You're right," Klaus said to Violet, and Sunny nodded in agreement. "We have to search the penthouse. But it's such a complicated place. I get lost just trying to find the bathroom at night. How can we search without getting lost?"

"Hansel!" Sunny said.

The two older Baudelaires looked at one another. It was rare that Sunny said something that her siblings couldn't understand, but this seemed to be one of those times.

"Do you mean we should draw a map?" Violet asked.

Sunny shook her head. "Gretel!" she said.

"That's two times we don't understand you," Klaus said. "Hansel and Gretel? What does that mean?"

"Oh!" Violet cried suddenly. "Hansel and Gretel means Hansel and Gretel—you know, those two dim-witted children in that fairy tale."

"Of course," Klaus said. "That brother and sister who insist on wandering around the woods by themselves."

"Leaving a trail of bread crumbs," Violet said, picking up a piece of toast from the breakfast tray Jerome had brought them, "so they don't get lost. We'll crumble up this toast and leave a few crumbs in every room so we know we've already searched it. Good thinking, Sunny."

"Blized," Sunny said modestly, which meant something like "It's nothing," and I'm sorry to say she turned out to be right. For as the children wandered from bedroom to living room to dining room to breakfast room to snack room to sitting room to standing room to ballroom to bathroom to kitchen to those rooms that seemed to have no purpose at all, and back again, leaving trails of toast crumbs wherever they went, Gunther was nowhere to be found. They looked in the closets of each bedroom, and the cabinets in each kitchen, and even pulled back the shower curtains in each bathroom to see if Gunther was hiding behind them. They saw racks of clothes in the closets, cans of food in the cabinets, and bottles of cream rinse in the shower, but the children had to admit, as the morning ended and the Baudelaires' own trail of crumbs led them back to Violet's room, that they had found nothing.

"Where in the world can Gunther be hiding?" Klaus asked. "We've looked everywhere."

"Maybe he was moving around," Violet said. "He could have been in a room behind us all the time, jumping into the hiding places we already checked."

"I don't think so," Klaus said. "We surely would have heard him if he was clomping around in those silly boots. I don't think he's been in this penthouse since last night. Esmé insists that he left the apartment, but the doorman insists that he didn't. It doesn't add up."

"I've been thinking that over," Violet said. "I think it might add up. Esmé insists that he left the *penthouse*. The doorman insists that he didn't leave the *building*. That means he could be in any of the other apartments at 667 Dark Avenue."

"You're right," Klaus said. "Maybe he rented one of the apartments on another floor, as a headquarters for his latest scheme."

"Or maybe one of the apartments belongs to someone in his theater troupe," Violet said, and counted those terrible people on her fingers "There's the hook-handed man, or the bald man with the long nose, or that one who looks like neither a man nor a woman."

"Or maybe those two dreadful powder-faced women—the ones who helped kidnap the Quagmires—are roommates," Klaus said.

"Co," Sunny said, which meant something like "Or maybe Gunther managed to trick one of the other residents of 667 Dark Avenue into letting him into their apartment, and then he tied them up and is sitting there hiding in the kitchen."

"If we find Gunther in the building," Violet said, "then at least the Squalors will know that he is a liar. Even if they don't believe he's really Count Olaf, they'll be very suspicious if he's caught hiding in another apartment."

"But how are we going to find out?" Klaus asked. "We can't simply knock on doors and ask to see each apartment."

"We don't have to *see* each apartment," Violet said. "We can *listen* to them."

Klaus and Sunny looked at their sister in confusion for a moment, and then began to grin. "You're right!" Klaus said. "If we walk down the stairs, listening at every door, we may be able to tell if Gunther is inside."

"Lorigo!" Sunny shrieked, which meant "What are we waiting for? Let's go!"

"Not so fast," Klaus said. "It's a long trip down all those stairs, and we've already done a lot of walking—and crawling, in your case, Sunny. We'd better change into our sturdiest shoes, and bring along some extra pairs of socks.

That way we can avoid blisters."

"And we should bring some water," Violet said, "so we won't get thirsty."

"Snack!" Sunny shrieked, and the Baudelaire orphans went to work, changing out of their pajamas and into appropriate stair-climbing outfits, putting on their sturdiest shoes, and tucking pairs of extra socks into their pockets. After Violet and Klaus made sure that Sunny had tied her shoes correctly, the children left their bedrooms and followed their crumbs down the hallway, through a living room, past two bedrooms, down another hallway, and into the nearest kitchen, sticking together the whole time so they wouldn't lose one another in the enormous penthouse. In the kitchen they found some grapes, a box of crackers, and a jar of apple butter, as well as a bottle of water that the Squalors used for making aqueous martinis but that the Baudelaires would use to quench their thirst during their long climb. Finally, they left the penthouse apartment, walked past the sliding elevator doors, and stood at the top of the curving stairway, feeling more like they were about to go mountain climbing than downstairs.

"We'll have to tiptoe," Violet said, "so that we can hear Gunther, but he can't hear us."

"And we should probably whisper," Klaus whispered, "so that we can eavesdrop, without people eavesdropping on us."

"Philavem," Sunny said, which meant "Let's get started," and the Baudelaires got started, tiptoeing down the first curve of the stairway and listening at the door of the apartment directly below the penthouse. For a few seconds, they heard nothing, but then, very clearly, they heard a woman talking on the phone.

"Well, that's not Gunther," Violet whispered. "He's not a woman."

Klaus and Sunny nodded, and the children tiptoed down the next curve to the floor below. As soon as they reached the next door, it flung open to reveal a very short man in a pinstripe suit. "See you later, Avery!" he called, and, with a nod to the children, shut the door and began walking down the stairs.

"That's not Gunther either," Klaus whispered. "He's not that short, and he's not calling himself Avery."

Violet and Sunny nodded, and the children tiptoed down the next curve to the floor below the floor below. They stopped and listened at this door, and heard a man's voice call out, "I'm going to take a shower, Mother," and Sunny shook her head.

"Mineak," she whispered, which meant "Gunther would never take a shower. He's filthy."

Violet and Klaus nodded, and the children tiptoed down the next curve, and then the next, and the next and plenty more after that, listening at each door, whispering briefly to one another, and moving on. As they walked farther and farther down the stairway, they began to grow tired, as they always did when making their way to or from the Squalors' apartment, but this time they had additional hardships as well. The tips of their toes grew tired from all that tiptoeing. Their throats grew hoarse from all that whispering. Their ears were aching from listening at all those doors, and their chins drooped from nodding in agreement that nothing they heard sounded like Gunther. The morning wore on, and the Baudelaires tiptoed and listened, whispered and nodded, and by the time they reached the lobby of the building, it seemed that every physical feature of the Baudelaire orphans was suffering in some way from the long climb.

"That was exhausting," Violet said, sitting down on the bottom step and passing around the bottle of water. "Exhausting and fruitless."

"Grape!" Sunny said.

"No, no, Sunny," Violet said. "I didn't mean we didn't have any fruit. I just meant we didn't learn anything. Do you think we missed a door?"

"No," Klaus said, shaking his head and passing around the crackers. "I made sure. I even counted the number of floors this time, so we could double-check them on the way up. It's not forty-eight, or eighty-four. It's sixty-six, which happens to be the average of those two numbers. Sixty-six floors and sixty-six doors and not a peep from Gunther behind any of them."

"I don't understand it," Violet said miserably. "If he's not in the penthouse, and he's not in any of the other apartments, and he hasn't left the building, where could he be?"

"Maybe he *is* in the penthouse," Klaus said, "and we just didn't spot him."

"Bishuy," Sunny said, which meant "Or maybe he *is* in one of the other apartments, and we just didn't hear him."

"Or maybe he *has* left the building," Violet said, spreading apple butter on a cracker and giving it to Sunny. "We can ask the doorman. There he is."

Sure enough, the doorman was at his usual post by the door, and was just noticing the three exhausted children sitting on the bottom step.

"Hello there," he said, walking up to them and smiling from beneath the wide brim of his hat. Sticking out of his long sleeves were a small starfish carved out of wood, and a bottle of glue. "I was just going to put up this ocean decoration when I thought I heard someone walking down the stairs."

"We just thought we'd have lunch here in the lobby," Violet said, not wanting to admit that she and her siblings had been listening at doors, "and then hike back up."

"I'm sorry, but that means that you're not allowed back up to the penthouse," the doorman said, and shrugged his shoulders inside his oversized coat. "You'll have to stay here in the lobby. After all, my instructions were very clear: You were not supposed to return to the Squalor penthouse until the guest left. I let you go up last night because Mr. Squalor said that your guest was probably on his way down, but he was wrong, because Gunther never showed up in the lobby."

"You mean Gunther still hasn't left the building?" Violet asked.

"Of course not," the doorman said. "I'm here all day and all night, and I haven't seen him leave. I promise you that Gunther never walked out of this door."

"When do you sleep?" Klaus asked.

"I drink a lot of coffee," the doorman answered.

"It just doesn't make any sense," Violet said.

"Sure it does," the doorman said. "Coffee contains caffeine, which is a chemical stimulant. Stimulants keep people awake."

"I didn't mean the part about the coffee," Violet said. "I meant the part about Gunther. Esmé—that's Mrs. Squalor—is positive that he left the penthouse last night, while we were at the restaurant. But you are equally positive that he didn't leave the building. It's a problem that doesn't seem to have a solution."

"Every problem has a solution," the doorman said. "At least, that's what a close associate of mine says. Sometimes it just takes a long time to find the solution—even if it's right in front of your nose."

The doorman smiled at the Baudelaires, who watched him walk over to the sliding elevator doors. He opened the bottle of glue and made a small globby patch on one of the doors, and then held the wooden starfish against the glue in order to attach it. Gluing things to a door is never a very exciting thing to watch, and after a moment, Violet and Sunny turned their attention back to their lunch and the problem of Gunther's disappearance. Only Klaus kept looking in the direction of the doorman as he continued to decorate the lobby. The middle Baudelaire looked and looked and looked, and kept on looking even when the glue dried and the doorman went back to his post at the door. Klaus kept facing the ocean decoration that was now firmly attached to one of the elevator doors, because he realized now, after a tiring morning of searching the penthouse and an exhausting afternoon of eavesdropping on the stairs, that the doorman had been right. Klaus didn't move his face one bit, because he realized that the solution was, indeed, right in front of his nose.

When you know someone a long time, you become accustomed to their idiosyncrasies, which is a fancy word for their unique habits. For instance, Sunny Baudelaire had known her sister, Violet, for quite some time, and was accustomed to Violet's idiosyncrasy of tying her hair up in a ribbon to keep it out of her eyes whenever she was inventing something. Violet had known Sunny for exactly the same length of time, and was accustomed to Sunny's idiosyncrasy of saying "Freijip?" when she wanted to ask the question "How can you think of elevators at a time like this?" And both the young Baudelaire women were very well acquainted with their brother, Klaus, and were accustomed to his idiosyncrasy of not paying a bit of attention to his surroundings when he was thinking very hard about something, as he was clearly doing as the afternoon wore on.

The doorman continued to insist that the Baudelaire orphans could not return to the penthouse, so the three children sat on the bottom step of 667 Dark Avenue's lengthy stairwell, ate food they had brought down with them, and rested their weary legs, which had not felt this sore since Olaf, in a previous disguise, had forced them to run hundreds and hundreds of laps as part of his scheme to steal their fortune. A good thing to do when one is sitting, eating, and resting is to have a conversation, and Violet and Sunny were both eager to converse about Gunther's mysterious appearance and disappearance, and what they might be able to do about it, but Klaus scarcely participated in the discussion. Only when his sisters asked him a direct question, such as "But where in the world could Gunther be?" or "What do you think Gunther is planning?" or "Topoing?" did Klaus mumble a response, and Violet and Sunny soon figured out that Klaus must be thinking very hard about something, so they left him to his idiosyncrasy and talked quietly to each other until the doorman ushered Jerome and Esmé into the lobby.

"Hello, Jerome," Violet said. "Hello, Esmé."

"Tretchev!" Sunny shrieked, which meant "Welcome home!"

Klaus mumbled something.

"What a pleasant surprise to see you all the way down here!" Jerome said. "It'll be easier to climb all those stairs if we have you three charming people for company."

"And you can carry the crates of parsley soda that are stacked outside," Esmé said. "Then I don't have to worry about breaking one of my fingernails."

"We'd be happy to carry big crates up all those stairs," Violet lied, "but the doorman says we're not allowed back in the penthouse."

"Not allowed?" Jerome frowned. "Whatever do you mean?"

"You gave me specific instructions not to let the children back in, Mrs. Squalor," the doorman said. "At least, until Gunther left the building. And he still hasn't left."

"Don't be absurd," Esmé said. "He left the penthouse last night. What kind of doorman are you?"

"Actually, I'm an actor," the doorman said, "but I was still able to follow your instructions."

Esmé gave the doorman a stern look she probably used when giving people financial advice. "Your instructions have changed," she said. "Your new instructions are to let me and my orphans go directly to my seventy-one-bedroom apartment. Got it, buster?"

"Got it," the doorman replied meekly.

"Good," Esmé said, and then turned to the

children. "Hurry up, kids," she said. "Violet and what's-his-name can each take a crate of soda, and Jerome will take the rest. I guess the baby won't be very helpful, but that's to be expected. Let's get a move on."

The Baudelaires got a move on, and in a few moments the three children and the two adults were trekking up the sixty-six-floor-long staircase. The youngsters were hoping that Esmé might help carry the heavy crates of soda, but the city's sixth most important financial advisor was much more interested in telling them all about her meeting with the King of Arizona than in buttering up any orphans. "He told me a long list of new things that are in," Esmé squealed. "For one thing, grapefruits. Also bright blue cereal bowls, billboards with photographs of weasels on them, and plenty of other things that I will list for you right now." All the way up to the penthouse, Esmé listed the new in items she had learned about from His Arizona Highness, and the two Baudelaire sisters listened carefully the whole time. They did not listen very carefully to Esmé's very dull speech, of course, but they listened closely at each curve of the staircase, double-checking their eavesdropping to hear if Gunther was indeed behind one of the apartment doors. Neither Violet nor Sunny heard anything suspicious, and they would have asked Klaus, in a low whisper so the Squalors couldn't hear them, if he had heard any sort of Gunther noise, but they could tell from his idiosyncrasy that he was still thinking very hard about something and wasn't listening to the noises in the other apartments any more than he was listening to automobile tires, cross-country skiing, movies with waterfalls in them, and the rest of the in things Esmé was rattling off.

"Oh, and magenta wallpaper!" Esmé said, as the Baudelaires and the Squalors finished a dinner of in foods washed down with parsley soda, which tasted even nastier than it sounds. "And triangular picture frames, and very fancy doilies, and garbage cans with letters of the alphabet stenciled all over them, and—"

"Excuse me," Klaus said, and his sisters jumped a little bit in surprise. It was the first time Klaus had spoken in anything but a mumble since they had been down in the lobby. "I don't mean to interrupt, but my sisters and I are very tired. May we be excused to go to bed?"

"Of course," Jerome said. "You should get plenty of rest for the auction tomorrow. I'll take you to the Veblen Hall at ten-thirty sharp, so—"

"No you won't," Esmé said. "Yellow paper clips are in, Jerome, so as soon as the sun rises, you'll have to go right to the Stationery District and get some. I'll bring the children."

"Well, I don't want to argue," Jerome said, shrugging and giving the children a small smile. "Esmé, don't you want to tuck the children in?"

"Nope," Esmé answered, frowning as she sipped her parsley soda. "Folding blankets over three wriggling children sounds like a lot more trouble than it's worth. See you tomorrow, kids."

"I hope so," Violet said, and yawned. She knew that Klaus was asking to be excused so he could tell her and Sunny what he had been thinking about, but after lying awake the previous night, searching the entire penthouse, and tiptoeing down all those stairs, the eldest Baudelaire was actually quite tired. "Good night, Esmé. Good night, Jerome."

"Good night, children," Jerome said. "And please, if you get up in the middle of the night and have a snack, try not to spill your food. There seem to be a lot of crumbs around the penthouse lately."

The Baudelaire orphans looked at one another and smiled at their shared secret. "Sorry about that," Violet said. "Tomorrow we'll do the vacuuming if you want."

"Vacuum cleaners!" Esmé said. "I knew there was something else he told me was in. Oh, and cotton balls, and anything with chocolate sprinkles on it, and . . ."

The Baudelaires did not want to stick around for any more of Esmé's in list, so they brought their plates into the nearest kitchen, and walked down a hallway decorated with the antlers of various animals, through a sitting room, past five bathrooms, took a left at another kitchen, and eventually made their way to Violet's bedroom.

"O.K., Klaus," Violet said to her brother, when the three children had found a comfortable corner for their discussion. "I know you've been thinking very hard about something, because you've been doing that unique habit of yours where you don't pay a bit of attention to your surroundings."

"Unique habits like that are called idiosyncrasies," Klaus said.

"Stiblo!" Sunny cried, which meant "We can improve our vocabulary later—tell us what's on your mind!"

"Sorry, Sunny," Klaus said. "It's just that I think I've figured out where Gunther might be hiding, but I'm not positive. First, Violet, I need to ask you something. What do you know about elevators?"

"Elevators?" Violet said. "Quite a bit, actually. My friend Ben once gave me some elevator blueprints for my birthday, and I studied them very closely. They were destroyed in the fire, of course, but I remember that an elevator is essentially a platform, surrounded by an enclosure, that moves along the vertical axis via an endlessly looped belt and a series of ropes. It's controlled by a push-button console that regulates an electromagnetic braking system so the transport sequence can be halted at any access point the passenger desires. In other words, it's a box that moves up or down, depending on where you want to go. But so what?"

"Freijip?" Sunny asked, which, as you know, was her idiosyncratic way of saying "How can you think of elevators at a time like this?"

"Well, it was the doorman who got me thinking about elevators," Klaus said. "Remember when he said that sometimes the solution is right under your nose? Well, he was gluing that wooden starfish to the elevator doors right when he said that."

"I noticed that, too," Violet said. "It looked a little ugly."

"It did look ugly," Klaus agreed. "But that's not what I mean. I got to thinking about the elevator doors. Outside the door to this penthouse, there are two pairs of elevator doors. But on every other floor, there's only one pair."

"That's true," Violet said, "and that's odd, too, now that I think of it. That means one elevator can stop only on the top floor."

"Yelliverc!" Sunny said, which meant "That second elevator is almost completely useless!"

"I don't think it's useless," Klaus said, "because I don't think the elevator is really there."

"Not really there?" Violet asked. "But that would just leave an empty elevator shaft!"

"Middiow?" Sunny asked.

"An elevator shaft is the path an elevator

uses to move up and down," Violet explained to her sister. "It's sort of like a hallway, except it goes up and down, instead of side to side."

"And a hallway," Klaus said, "could lead to a hiding place."

"Aha!" Sunny cried.

"Aha is right," Klaus agreed. "Just think, if he used an empty elevator shaft instead of the stairs, nobody would ever know where he was. I don't think the elevator has been shut down because it's out. I think it's where Gunther is hiding."

"But why is he hiding? What is he up to?" Violet asked.

"That's the part we still don't know," Klaus admitted, "but I bet you the answers can be found behind those sliding doors. Let's take a look at what's behind the second pair of elevator doors. If we see the ropes and things you were describing, then we know it's a real elevator. But if we don't—"

"Then we know we're on the right track,"

Violet finished for him. "Let's go right this minute."

"If we go right this minute," Klaus said, "we'll have do it very quietly. The Squalors are not going to let three children poke around an elevator shaft."

"It's worth the risk, if it helps us figure out Gunther's plan," Violet said. I'm sorry to say that it turned out not to be worth the risk at all, but of course the Baudelaires had no way of knowing that, so they merely nodded in agreement and tiptoed toward the penthouse's exit, peeking into each room before they went through to see if the Squalors were anywhere to be found. But Jerome and Esmé were apparently spending the evening in some room in another part of the apartment, because the Baudelaires didn't see hide or hair of them—the expression "hide or hair of them" here means "even a glimpse of the city's sixth most important financial advisor, or her husband"—on their way to the front door. They hoped the door would not squeak as they pushed it open, but apparently silent hinges were in, because the Baudelaires made no noise at all as they left the apartment and tiptoed over to the two pairs of sliding elevator doors.

"How do we know which elevator is which?" Violet whispered. "The pairs of doors look exactly alike."

"I hadn't thought of that," Klaus replied. "If one of them is really a secret passageway, there must be some way to tell."

Sunny tugged on the legs of her siblings' pants, which was a good way to get their attention without making any noise, and when Violet and Klaus looked down to see what their sister wanted, she answered them just as silently. Without speaking, she reached out one of her tiny fingers and pointed to the buttons that were next to each set of sliding doors. Next to one pair of doors, there was a single button, with an arrow printed on it pointing down. But next to the second pair of doors, there were two buttons: one with a Down arrow, and one with an Up arrow. The three children looked at the buttons and considered.

"Why would you need an Up button," Violet whispered, "if you were already on the top floor?" and without waiting for an answer to her question, she reached out and pressed it. With a quiet, slithery sound, the sliding doors opened, and the children leaned carefully into the doorway, and gasped at what they saw.

"Lakry," Sunny said, which meant something like "There are no ropes."

"Not only are there no ropes," Violet said. "There's no endlessly looped belt, push-button console, or electromagnetic braking system. I don't even see an enclosed platform."

"I *knew* it," Klaus said, in hushed excitement. "I *knew* the elevator was ersatz!"

"Ersatz" is a word that describes a situation in which one thing is pretending to be another, the way the secret passageway the Baudelaires were looking at had been pretending to be an elevator, but the word might as well have meant "the most terrifying place the Baudelaires had ever seen." As the children stood in the doorway and peered into the elevator shaft, it was as if they were standing on the edge of an enormous cliff, looking down at the dizzying depths below them. But what made these depths terrifying, as well as dizzying, was that they were so very dark. The shaft was more like a pit than a passageway, leading straight down into a blackness the likes of which the youngsters had never seen. It was darker than any night had ever been, even on nights when there was no moon. It was darker than Dark Avenue had been on the day of their arrival. It was darker than a pitch-black panther, covered in tar, eating black licorice at the very bottom of the deepest part of the Black Sea. The Baudelaire orphans had never dreamed that anything could be this dark, even in their scariest nightmares, and as they stood at the edge of this pit of unimaginable blackness, they felt as if the elevator shaft would simply swallow them up and they would never see a speck of light again.

"We have to go down there," Violet said, scarcely believing the words she was saying.

"I'm not sure I have the courage to go down there," Klaus said. "Look how dark it is. It's terrifying."

"Prollit," Sunny said, which meant "But not as terrifying as what Gunther will do to us, if we don't find out his plan."

"Why don't we just go tell the Squalors about this?" Klaus asked. "Then *they* can go down the secret passageway."

"We don't have time to argue with the Squalors," Violet said. "Every minute we waste is a minute the Quagmires are spending in Gunther's clutches."

"But how are we going to go down?" Klaus asked. "I don't see a ladder, or a staircase. I don't see anything at all."

"We're going to have to climb down," Violet said, "on a rope. But where can we find rope at this time of night? Most hardware stores close at six."

"The Squalors must have some rope somewhere in their penthouse," Klaus said. "Let's split up and find some. We'll meet back here in fifteen minutes."

Violet and Sunny agreed, and the Baudelaires stepped carefully away from the elevator shaft and tiptoed back into the Squalor penthouse. They felt like burglars as they split up and began searching the apartment, although there have been only five burglars in the history of robbery who have specialized in rope. All five of these burglars were caught and sent to prison, which is why scarcely any people lock up their rope for safekeeping, but to their frustration, the Baudelaires learned that their guardians didn't lock up their ropes at all, for the simple reason that they didn't have any.

"I couldn't find any ropes at all," Violet admitted, as she rejoined her siblings. "But I did find these extension cords, which might work."

"I took these curtain pulls down from some of the windows," Klaus said. "They're a little bit like ropes, so I thought they might be useful."

"Armani," Sunny offered, holding up an armful of Jerome's neckties.

"Well, we have some ersatz ropes," Violet said, "for our climb down the ersatz elevator. Let's tie them all together with the Devil's Tongue."

"The Devil's Tongue?" Klaus asked.

"It's a knot," Violet explained. "It was invented by female Finnish pirates in the fifteenth century. I used it to make my grappling hook, when Olaf had Sunny trapped in that cage, dangling from his tower room, and it'll work here as well. We need to make as long a rope as possible—for all we know, the passageway goes all the way to the bottom floor of the building."

"It looks like it goes all the way to the center of the earth," Klaus said. "We've spent so much of our time trying to escape from Count Olaf. I can't believe that now we're trying to find him."

"Me neither," Violet agreed. "If it weren't for the Quagmires, I wouldn't go down there at all."

"Bangemp," Sunny reminded her siblings. She meant something along the lines of "If it weren't for the Quagmires, we would have been in his clutches a long time ago," and the two older Baudelaires nodded in agreement. Violet showed her siblings how to make the Devil's Tongue, and the three children hurriedly tied the extension cords to the curtain pulls, and the curtain pulls to the neckties, and the last necktie to the sturdiest thing they could find, which was the doorknob of the Squalor penthouse. Violet checked her siblings' handiwork and finally gave the whole rope a satisfied tug.

"I think this should hold us," she said. "I only hope it's long enough."

"Why don't we drop the rope down the shaft," Klaus said, "and listen to see if it hits the bottom? Then we'll know for sure."

"Good idea," Violet replied, and walked to the edge of the passageway. She threw down the edge of the furthermost extension cord, and the children watched as it disappeared into the blackness, dragging the rest of the Baudelaires' line with it. The coils of cord and pull and necktie unwound quickly, like a long snake waking up and slithering down into the shaft. It slithered and slithered and slithered, and the children leaned forward as far as they dared and listened as hard as they could. Finally, they heard a faint, faint *clink!*, as if the extension cord had hit a piece of metal, and the three orphans looked at one another. The thought of climbing down all that distance in the dark, on an ersatz rope they had fashioned themselves, made them want to turn around and run all the way back to their beds and pull the blankets over their heads. The siblings stood together at the edge of this dark and terrible place and wondered if they really dared to begin the climb.

The Baudelaire rope had made it to the bottom.
But would the Baudelaire children?

"Are you ready?" Klaus asked finally.

"No," Sunny answered.

"Me neither," Violet said, "but if we wait
until we're ready we'll be waiting for the rest of
our lives. Let's go."

Violet tugged one last time on the rope, and
carefully, carefully lowered herself down the
passageway. Klaus and Sunny watched her
disappear into the darkness as if some huge,
hungry creature had eaten her up. "Come on,"
they heard her whisper, from the blackness.
"It's O.K."

Klaus blew on his hands, and Sunny blew on
hers, and the two younger Baudelaires followed
their sister into the utter darkness of the elevator shaft, only to discover that Violet had not
told the truth. It was not O.K. It was not half
O.K. It was not even one twenty-seventh O.K.
The climb down the shadowy passageway felt
like falling into a deep hole at the bottom of a

deep pit on the bottom floor of a dungeon that was deep underground, and it was the least O.K. situation the Baudelaires had ever encountered. Their hands gripping the line was the only thing they saw, because even as their eyes adjusted to the darkness, they were afraid to look anywhere else, particularly down. The distant *clink!* at the bottom of the line was the only sound they heard, because the Baudelaires were too scared to speak. And the only thing they felt was sheer terror, as deep and as dark as the passageway itself, a terror so profound that I have slept with four night-lights ever since I visited 667 Dark Avenue and saw this deep pit that the Baudelaires climbed down. But I also saw, during my visit, what the Baudelaire orphans saw when they reached the bottom after climbing for more than three terrifying hours. By then, their eyes had adjusted to the darkness, and they could see what the bottom of their line was hitting, when it was making that faint clinking sound. The edge of the farthest extension cord was bumping up against a piece of metal, all right—a metal lock. The lock was secured around a metal door, and the metal door was attached to a series of metal bars that made up a rusty metal cage. By the time my research led me to this passageway, the cage was empty, and had been empty for a very long time. But it was not empty when the Baudelaires reached it. As they arrived at the bottom of this deep and terrifying place, the Baudelaire orphans looked into the cage and saw the huddled and trembling figures of Duncan and Isadora Quagmire.

"I'm dreaming," Duncan Quagmire said. His voice was a hoarse whisper of utter shock. "I must be dreaming."

"But how can you be dreaming," Isadora asked him, "if I'm having the same dream?"

"I once read about a journalist," Duncan whispered, "who was reporting on a war and was imprisoned by the enemy for three years. Each morning, she looked out her cell window and thought she saw her grandparents coming to rescue her. But they weren't really there. It was a hallucination."

"I remember reading about a poet," Isadora

said, "who would see six lovely maidens in his kitchen on Tuesday nights, but his kitchen was really empty. It was a phantasm."

"No," Violet said, and reached her hand between the bars of the cage. The Quagmire triplets shrank back into the cage's far corner, as if Violet were a poisonous spider instead of a long-lost friend. "It's not a hallucination. It's me, Violet Baudelaire."

"And it's really Klaus," Klaus said. "I'm not a phantasm."

"Sunny!" Sunny said.

The Baudelaire orphans blinked in the darkness, straining their eyes to see as much as possible. Now that they were no longer dangling from the end of a rope, they were able to get a good look at their gloomy surroundings. Their long climb ended in a tiny, filthy room with nothing in it but the rusty cage that the extension cord had clinked against, but the Baudelaires saw that the passageway continued with a long hallway, just as shadowy as the elevator shaft, that twisted and turned away into the dark. The children also got a good look at the Quagmires, and that view was no less gloomy. They were dressed in tattered rags, and their faces were so smeared with dirt that the Baudelaires might not have recognized them, if the two triplets had not been holding the notebooks they took with them wherever they went. But it was not just the dirt on their faces, or the clothes on their bodies, that made the Quagmires look so different. It was the look in their eyes. The Quagmire triplets looked exhausted, and they looked hungry, and they looked very, very frightened. But most of all, Isadora and Duncan looked haunted. The word "haunted," I'm sure you know, usually applies to a house, graveyard, or supermarket that has ghosts living in it, but the word can also be used to describe people who have seen and heard such horrible things that they feel as if ghosts are living inside them, haunting their brains and hearts with misery and despair. The Quagmires looked this way, and it broke the Baudelaire hearts to see their friends look so desperately sad.

"Is it really you?" Duncan said, squinting at the Baudelaires from the far end of the cage. "Can it really, really be you?"

"Oh, yes," Violet said, and found that her eyes were filling with tears.

"It's really the Baudelaires," Isadora said, stretching her hand out to meet Violet's. "We're not dreaming, Duncan. They're really here."

Klaus and Sunny reached into the cage as well, and Duncan left his corner to reach the Baudelaires as best he could from behind bars. The five children embraced as much as they could, half laughing and half crying because they were all together once more.

"How in the world did you know where we are?" Isadora said. "*We* don't even know where we are."

"You're in a secret passageway inside 667 Dark Avenue," Klaus said, "but we didn't know you'd be here. We were just trying to find out what Gunther—that's what Olaf is calling himself now—was up to, and our search led us all the way down here."

"I know what he's calling himself," Duncan said, "and I know what he's up to." He shuddered, and opened his notebook, which the Baudelaires remembered was dark green but looked black in the gloom. "Every second we spend with him, all he does is brag about his horrible plans, and when he's not looking, I write down everything he tells us so I don't forget it. Even though I'm a kidnap victim, I'm still a journalist."

"And I'm still a poet," Isadora said, and opened her notebook, which the Baudelaires remembered was black, but now looked even blacker. "Listen to this:

"On Auction Day, when the sun goes down,
Gunther will sneak us out of town."

"How will he do that?" Violet asked. "The

police have been informed of your kidnapping, and are on the lookout."

"I know," Duncan said. "Gunther wants to smuggle us out of the city, and hide us away on some island where the police won't find us. He'll keep us on the island until we come of age and he can steal the Quagmire sapphires. Once he has our fortune, he says, he'll take us and—"

"Don't say it," Isadora cried, covering her ears. "He's told us so many horrible things. I can't stand to hear them again."

"Don't worry, Isadora," Klaus said. "We'll alert the authorities, and they'll arrest him before he can do anything."

"But it's almost too late," Duncan said. "The In Auction is tomorrow morning. He's going to hide us inside one of the items and have one of his associates place the highest bid."

"Which item?" Violet asked.

Duncan flipped the pages of his notebook, and his eyes widened as he reread some of the wretched things Gunther had said. "I don't know," he said. "He's told us so many haunting secrets, Violet. So many awful schemes—all the treachery he has done in the past, and all he's planning to do in the future. It's all here in this notebook—from V.F.D. all the way to this terrible auction plan."

"We'll have plenty of time to discuss everything," Klaus said, "but in the meantime, let's get you out of this cage before Gunther comes back. Violet, do you think you can pick this lock?"

Violet took the lock in her hands and squinted at it in the gloom. "It's pretty complicated," she said. "He must have bought himself some extra-difficult locks, after I broke into that suitcase of his when we were living with Uncle Monty. If I had some tools, maybe I could invent something, but there's absolutely nothing down here."

"Aguen?" Sunny asked, which meant something like "Could you saw through the bars of the cage?"

"Not saw," Violet said, so quietly that it was as if she was talking to herself. "I don't have the time to manufacture a saw. But maybe . . ." Her voice trailed off, but the other children could see, in the gloom, that she was tying her hair up in a ribbon, to keep it out of her eyes.

"Look, Duncan," Isadora said, "she's thinking up an invention! We'll be out of here in no time!"

"Every night since we've been kidnapped," Duncan said, "we've been dreaming of the day when we would see Violet Baudelaire inventing something that could rescue us."

"If we're going to rescue you in time," Violet said, thinking furiously, "then my siblings and I have to climb back up to the penthouse right away."

Isadora looked nervously around the tiny, dark room. "You're going to leave us alone?" she asked.

"If I'm going to invent something to get you out of that cage," Violet replied, "I need all the help I can get, so Klaus and Sunny have to come with me. Sunny, start climbing. Klaus and I will be right behind you."

"Onosew," Sunny said, which meant "Yes ma'am," and Klaus lifted her up to the end of the rope so she could begin the long, dark climb back up to the Squalors' apartment. Klaus began climbing right behind her, and Violet clasped hands with her friends.

"We'll be back as soon as we can," she promised. "Don't worry, Quagmires. You'll be out of danger before you know it."

"In case anything goes wrong," Duncan said, flipping to a page in his notebook, "like it did the last time, let me tell you—"

Violet placed her finger on Duncan's mouth. "Shush," she said. "Nothing will go wrong this time. I swear it."

"But if it does," Duncan said, "you should know about V.F.D. before the auction begins."

"Don't tell me about it now," Violet said. "We don't have time. You can tell us when we're all safe and sound." The eldest Baudelaire grabbed the end of the extension cord and started to follow her siblings. "I'll see you soon," she called down to the Quagmires, who were already fading into the darkness as she began her climb. "I'll see you soon," she said again, just as she lost all sight of them.

The climb back up the secret passageway was much more tiring but a lot less terrifying, simply because they knew what they would find at the other end of their ersatz rope. On the way down the elevator shaft, the Baudelaires had no idea what would be waiting for them at the bottom of such a dark and cavernous journey, but Violet, Klaus, and Sunny knew that all seventy-one bedrooms of the Squalor penthouse would be at the top. And it was these bedrooms—along with the living rooms, dining rooms, breakfast rooms, snack rooms, sitting rooms, standing rooms, ballrooms, bathrooms, kitchens, and the assortment of rooms that seemed to have no purpose at all—that would be helpful in rescuing the Quagmires.

"Listen to me," Violet said to her siblings, after they had been climbing for a few minutes. "When we get up to the top, I want the two of you to search the penthouse."

"What?" Klaus said, peering down at his sister. "We already searched it yesterday, remember?"

"I don't want you to search it for Gunther," Violet replied. "I want you to search it for long, slender objects made of iron."

"Agoula?" Sunny asked, which meant "What for?"

"I think the easiest way to get the Quagmires out of that cage will be by welding," Violet said. "Welding is when you use something very hot to melt metal. If we melt through a few of the bars of the cage, we can make a door and get Duncan and Isadora out of there."

"That's a good idea," Klaus agreed. "But I thought that welding required a lot of complicated equipment."

"Usually it does," Violet said. "In a normal welding situation, I'd use a welding torch, which is a device that makes a very small flame to melt the metal. But the Squalors won't have a welding torch—that's a tool, and tools are out. So I'm going to devise another method. When you two find the long, slender objects made of iron, meet me in the kitchen closest to the front door."

"Selrep," Sunny said, which meant something like "That's the one with the bright blue oven."

"Right," Violet said, "and I'm going to use that bright blue oven to heat those iron objects as hot as they can get. When they are burning, burning hot, we will take them back down to the cage and use their heat to melt the bars."

"Will they stay hot long enough to work, after such a long climb down?" Klaus asked.

"They'd better," Violet replied grimly. "It's our only hope."

To hear the phrase "our only hope" always makes one anxious, because it means that if the only hope doesn't work, there is nothing left, and that is never pleasant to think about, however true it might be. The three Baudelaires felt anxious about the fact that Violet's invention was their only hope of rescuing the Quagmires, and they were quiet the rest of the way up the elevator shaft, not wanting to consider what would happen to Duncan and Isadora if this only hope didn't work. Finally, they began to see the dim light from the open sliding doors, and at last they were once again at the front door of the Squalors' apartment.

"Remember," Violet whispered, "long, slender objects made of iron. We can't use bronze or silver or even gold, because those metals will melt in the oven. I'll see you in the kitchen."

The younger Baudelaires nodded solemnly, and followed two different trails of bread crumbs in opposite directions, while Violet walked straight into the kitchen with the bright blue oven and looked around uncertainly. Cooking had never been her forte—a phrase which here means "something she couldn't do very well, except for making toast, and sometimes she couldn't even do that without burning it to a crisp"—and she was a bit nervous about using the oven without any adult supervision. But then she thought about all the things she had done recently without adult supervision—sprinkling crumbs on the floor, eating apple butter, climbing down an empty elevator shaft on a ersatz rope made of extension cords, curtain pulls, and neckties tied together with the Devil's Tongue—and stiffened her resolve. She turned the oven's bright blue temperature dial to the highest temperature—500 degrees Fahrenheit—and then, as the oven slowly heated up, began quietly opening and closing the kitchen drawers, looking for three sturdy oven mitts. Oven mitts, as you probably know, are kitchen accessories that serve as ersatz hands by enabling you to pick up objects that would burn your fingers if you touched them directly. The Baudelaires would have to use oven mitts, Violet realized, once the long, slender objects were hot enough to be used as welding torches. Just as her siblings entered the kitchen, Violet found three oven mitts emblazoned with the fancy, curly writing of the In Boutique stuffed into the bottom of the ninth drawer she had opened.

"We hit the jackpot," Klaus whispered, and Sunny nodded in agreement. The two younger Baudelaires were using an expression which here means "Look at these fire tongs—they're perfect!" and they were absolutely right. "Fireplaces must have been in at some point," Klaus explained, holding up three long, slender pieces of iron, "because Sunny remembered that living room with six fireplaces between the ballroom with the green walls and the bathroom with that funny-looking sink. Next to the fireplaces are fire tongs—you know, these long pieces of iron that people use to move logs around to keep a fire going. I figured that if they can touch burning logs, they'll be able to survive a hot oven."

"You really did hit the jackpot," Violet said. "Fire tongs are perfect. Now, when I open the door of the oven, you put them in, Klaus. Sunny, stand back. Babies shouldn't be near a hot oven."

"Prawottle," Sunny said. She meant something like "Older children aren't supposed to be near a hot oven either, especially without adult supervision," but she understood that it was an emergency and crawled to the opposite end of the kitchen, where she could safely watch her older siblings put the long, slender tongs into the hot oven. Like most ovens, the Squalors' bright blue oven was designed for baking cakes and casseroles, not fire tongs, and it was impossible to shut the door of the oven with the long pieces of iron inside. So, as the Baudelaire orphans waited for the pieces of iron to heat up into welding torches, the kitchen heated up as well, as some of the hot air from the oven escaped out the open door. By the time Klaus asked if the welding torches were ready, the kitchen felt as if it were an oven instead of merely containing one.

"Not yet," Violet replied, peering carefully into the open oven door. "The tips of the tongs are just beginning to get yellow with heat. We need them to get white with heat, so it will still be a few minutes."

"I'm nervous," Klaus said, and then corrected himself. "I mean I'm *anxious*. I don't like leaving the Quagmires down there all alone."

"I'm anxious, too," Violet said, "but the only thing we can do now is wait. If we take the iron out of the oven now, it won't be of any use to us by the time we get all the way down to the cage."

Klaus and Sunny sighed, but they nodded in agreement with their sister and settled down to wait for the welding torches to be ready, and as they waited, they felt as if this particular kitchen in the Squalor penthouse was being remodeled before their very eyes. When the Baudelaires had searched the apartment to see if Gunther was hiding in it, they had left crumbs in an assortment of bedrooms, living rooms, dining rooms, breakfast rooms, snack rooms, sitting rooms, standing rooms, bathrooms, ballrooms, and kitchens, as well as those rooms that seemed to have no purpose at all, but the one type of room that the Squalor penthouse lacked was a waiting room. Waiting rooms, as I'm sure you know, are small rooms with plenty of chairs for waiting, as well as piles of old, dull magazines to read and some vapid paintings—the word "vapid" here means "usually containing horses in a field or puppies in a basket"—while you endure the boredom that doctors and dentists inflict on their patients before bringing them in to poke them and prod them and do all the miserable things that such people are paid to do. It is very rare to have a waiting room in someone's home, because even a home as enormous as the Squalors' does not contain a doctor's or dentist's office, and also because waiting rooms are so uninteresting that you would never want one in the place where you live. The Baudelaires had certainly never wished that the Squalors had a waiting room in their penthouse, but as they sat and waited for Violet's invention to be ready to use, they felt as if waiting rooms were suddenly in and Esmé had ordered one constructed right there in the kitchen. The kitchen cabinets were not painted with horses in a field or puppies in a basket, and there were no old, dull magazine articles printed on the bright blue stove, but as the three children waited for the iron objects to turn yellow and then orange and then red as they grew hotter and hotter and hotter, they felt the same itchy nervousness as they did when waiting for a trained medical professional.

But at last the fire tongs were white-hot, and were ready for their welding appointment with the thick iron bars of the cage. Violet passed out an oven mitt to each of her siblings and then put the third one on her own hand to carefully remove each tong from the oven. "Hold them very, very carefully," she said, giving an ersatz welding torch to each of her siblings. "They're hot enough to melt metal, so just imagine what they could do if they touched us. But I'm sure we can manage."

"It'll be tougher to go down this time," Klaus said, as he followed his sisters to the front door of the penthouse. He held his fire tong straight up, as if it were a regular torch instead of a welding one, and he kept his eye on the white-hot part so that it wouldn't brush up against anything or anybody. "We'll each have to keep one hand free to hold the torch. But I'm sure we can manage."

"Zelestin," Sunny said, when the children reached the sliding doors of the ersatz elevator. She meant something along the lines of "It'll be terrifying to climb down that horrible passageway again," but after she said "Zelestin" she added the word "Enipy," which meant "But I'm sure we can manage," and the youngest Baudelaire was as sure as her siblings. The three children stood at the edge of the dark passageway, but they did not pause to gather their courage, as they had done before their first descent into the gaping shaft. Their welding torches were hot, as Violet had said, and going down would be tough, as Klaus had said, and the climb would be terrifying, as Sunny had said, but the siblings looked at one another and knew they could manage. The Quagmire triplets were counting on them, and the Baudelaire orphans were sure that this only hope would work after all.

CHAPTER Nine

One of the greatest myths in the world—
and the phrase "greatest myths" is just a
fancy way of saying "big fat lies"—is that
troublesome things get less and less
troublesome if you do them more and
more. People say this myth when they
are teaching children to ride bicycles,
for instance, as though falling off a
bicycle and skinning your knee is less
troublesome the fourteenth time you
do it than it is the first time. The truth

is that troublesome things tend to remain troublesome no matter how many times you do
them, and that you should avoid doing them
unless they are absolutely urgent.

Obviously, it was absolutely urgent for the
Baudelaire orphans to take another three-hour
climb down into the terrible darkness of the
elevator shaft. The children knew that the
Quagmire triplets were in grave danger, and that
using Violet's invention to melt the bars of the
cage was the only way that their friends could
escape before Gunther hid them inside one of
the items of the In Auction, and smuggled them
out of the city. But I'm sorry to say that the
absolute urgency of the Baudelaires' second
climb did not make it any less troublesome.
The passageway was still as dark as a bar of
extra-dark chocolate sitting in a planetarium
covered in a thick, black blanket, even with
the tiny glow from the white-hot tips of the fire
tongs, and the sensation of lowering themselves down the elevator shaft still felt like a

descent into the hungry mouth of some terrible creature. With only the *clink!* of the last extension cord hitting the lock of the cage to guide them, the three siblings pulled themselves down the ersatz rope with one hand, and held out their welding torches with the other, and the trek down to the tiny, filthy room where the triplets were trapped was still not even one twenty-seventh O.K.

But the dreadful repetition of the Baudelaires' troublesome climb was dwarfed in comparison with the sinister surprise they found at the bottom, a surprise so terrible that the three children simply refused to believe it. Violet reached the end of the final extension cord and thought it was a hallucination. Klaus stood looking at the cage and thought that it must be a phantasm. And Sunny peered in through the bars and prayed that it was some combination of the two. The youngsters stared at the tiny, filthy room, and stared at the cage, but it took them several minutes before they believed that the Quagmires were no longer inside.

"They're gone," Violet said. "They're gone, and it's all my fault!" She threw her welding torch into the corner of the tiny room, where it sizzled against the floor. She turned to her siblings, and they could see, by the white glow of their tongs, that their older sister was beginning to cry. "My invention was supposed to save them," she said mournfully, "and now Gunther has snatched them away. I'm a terrible inventor, and a horrible friend."

Klaus threw his welding torch into the corner, and gave his sister a hug. "You're the best inventor I know," he said, "and your invention was a good one. Listen to those welding torches sizzle. The time just wasn't ripe for your invention, that's all."

"What's that supposed to mean?" Violet said miserably.

Sunny threw the last welding torch into the corner, and took off her oven mitt so she could pat her sister comfortingly on the ankle. "Noque, noque," she said, which meant "There, there."

"All it means," Klaus said, "is that you invented something that wasn't handy at this particular time. It's not your fault that we didn't rescue them—it's Gunther's."

"I guess I know that," Violet said, wiping her eyes. "I'm just sad that the time wasn't ripe for my invention. Who knows if we will ever see our friends again?"

"We will," Klaus said. "Just because the time isn't right for your inventing skills, doesn't meant it isn't ripe for my researching skills."

"Dwestall," Sunny said sadly, which meant "All the research in the world can't help Duncan and Isadora now."

"That's where you're wrong, Sunny," Klaus replied. "Gunther might have snatched them, but we know where he's taking them—to Veblen Hall. He's going to hide them inside one of the items at the In Auction, remember?"

"Yes," Violet said, "but which one?"

"If we climb back up to the penthouse," Klaus said, "and go to the Squalor library, I think I can figure it out."

"Meotze," Sunny said, which meant "But the Squalor library has only those snooty books on what's in and what's out."

"You're forgetting the recent addition to the library," Klaus said. "Esmé told us that Gunther had left a copy of the In Auction catalog, remember? Wherever he's planning to hide the Quagmires, it'll be listed in the catalog. If we can figure out which item he's hiding them in—"

"We can get them out of there," Violet finished, "before he auctions them off. That's a brilliant idea, Klaus!"

"It's no less brilliant than inventing welding torches," Klaus said. "I just hope the time is ripe this time."

"Me too," Violet said. "After all, it's our only—"

"Vinung," Sunny said, which meant "Don't say it," and her sister nodded in agreement. There was no use in saying it was their only hope, and getting them as anxious as they were before, so without another word the Baudelaires hoisted themselves back up on their makeshift rope and began climbing back up to the Squalor penthouse. The darkness closed in on them again, and the children began to feel as if their whole lives had been spent in this deep and shadowy pit, instead of in a variety of locations ranging from a lumbermill in Paltryville to a cave on the shores of Lake Lachrymose to the Baudelaire mansion, which sat in charred remains just a few blocks away from Dark Avenue. But rather than think about all of the shadowy places in the Baudelaire past, or the shadowiest place that they were climbing through now, the three siblings tried to concentrate on the brighter places in the Baudelaire future. They thought of the penthouse apartment, which drew closer and closer to them as they climbed.

They thought of the Squalor library, which could contain the proper information they needed to defeat Gunther's plan. And they thought of some glorious time that was yet to come, when the Baudelaires and the Quagmires could enjoy their friendship without the ghastly shadow of evil and greed that hung over them now. The Baudelaire orphans tried to keep their minds on these bright thoughts of the future as they climbed up the shadowy elevator shaft, and by the time they reached the sliding doors they felt that perhaps this glorious time was not so far off.

"It must almost be morning," Violet said, as she helped Sunny hoist herself out of the elevator doors. "We'd better untie our rope from the doorknob, and shut these doors, otherwise the Squalors will see what we've been up to."

"Why shouldn't they see?" Klaus asked. "Maybe then they'd believe us about Gunther."

"No one ever believes us about Gunther, or any of Olaf's other disguises," Violet said, "unless we have some evidence. All we have now is an ersatz elevator, an empty cage, and three cooling fire tongs. That's not evidence of anything."

"I suppose you're right," Klaus said. "Well, why don't you two untie the rope, and I'll go straight to the library and start reading the catalog."

"Good plan," Violet said.

"Reauhop!" Sunny said, which meant "And good luck!" Klaus quietly opened the door of the penthouse and let himself in, and the Baudelaire sisters began pulling the rope back up the shaft. The end of the last extension cord *clink*ed and *clink*ed against the walls of the passageway as Sunny wound up the ersatz rope until it was a coil of extension cords, curtain pulls, and fancy neckties. Violet untied the last double knot to detach it from the doorknob, and turned to her sister.

"Let's store this under my bed," she said, "in case we need it later. It's on the way to the library anyway."

"Yallrel," Sunny added, which meant "And let's shut the sliding elevator doors, so the Squalors don't see that we've been sneaking around an elevator shaft."

"Good thinking," Violet said, and pressed the Up button. The doors slid shut again, and after taking a good look around to make sure they hadn't left anything behind, the two Baudelaires walked into the penthouse and followed their bread-crumb trail past a breakfast room, down a hallway, across a standing room, down a hallway, and finally to Violet's room, where they stored the ersatz rope under the bed. They were about to head right to the library when Sunny noticed a note that had been left on Violet's extra-fluffy pillow.

"'Dear Violet,'" read Violet, "'I couldn't find you or your siblings this morning to say good-bye. I had to leave early to buy yellow paper clips before heading over to the In Auction. Esmé will take you to Veblen Hall at ten-thirty sharp, so be sure to be ready, or she'll be very annoyed. See you then! Sincerely yours, Jerome Squalor.'"

"Yikes!" Sunny said, pointing to the nearest of the 612 clocks that the Squalors owned.

"Yikes is right," Violet said. "It's already ten o'clock. All that climbing up and down the elevator shaft took much longer than I thought."

"Wrech," Sunny added, which meant something like "Not to mention making those welding torches."

"We'd better go to the library right away," Violet said. "Maybe we can help Klaus speed up the research process in some way."

Sunny nodded in agreement, and the two sisters walked down the hallway to the Squalor library. Since Jerome had first shown it to them, Violet and Sunny had scarcely been inside, and it looked like nobody else had used it much, either. A good library will never be too neat, or too dusty, because somebody will always be in it, taking books off the shelves and staying up late reading them. Even libraries that were not to the Baudelaires' taste—Aunt Josephine's library, for instance, only contained books on grammar—were comfortable places to be in, because the owners of the library used them so much. But the Squalor library was as neat and as dusty as could be. All of the dull books on what was in and what was out sat on the shelves in tidy rows, with layers of dust on top of them as if they hadn't been disturbed since they'd first been placed there. It made the Baudelaire sisters a little sad to see all those books sitting in the library unread and unnoticed, like stray dogs or lost children that nobody wanted to take home. The only sign of life in the library was their brother, who was reading the catalog so closely that he didn't look up until his sisters were standing at his side.

"I hate to disturb you when you're researching," Violet said, "but there was a note from Jerome on my pillow. Esmé is going to take us to Veblen Hall at ten-thirty sharp, and it's just past ten o'clock now. Is there any way we can help you?"

"I don't see how," Klaus said, his eyes look-ing worried behind his glasses. "There's only one copy of the catalog, and it's pretty compli-cated. Each of the items for the auction is called a lot, and the catalog lists each lot with a de-scription and a guess at what the highest bid may be. I've read up to Lot #49, which is a valu-able postage stamp."

"Well, Gunther can't hide the Quagmires in a postage stamp," Violet said. "You can skip that lot."

"I've been skipping lots of lots," Klaus said, "but I'm still no closer to figuring out where the triplets will be. Would Gunther hide them in Lot #14—an enormous globe? Would he hide them under the lid of Lot #25—a rare and valu-able piano? Would he hide them in Lot #48—an enormous statue of a scarlet fish?" Klaus stopped and turned the page of a catalog. "Or would he hide them in Lot #50, which is—"

Klaus ended his sentence in a gasp, but his sisters knew immediately that he did not mean that the fiftieth item to be sold at the In Auction was a sharp intake of breath. He meant he'd discovered something remarkable in the catalog, and they leaned forward to read over his shoulder and see what it was.

"I can't believe it," Violet said. "I simply can't believe it."

"Toomsk," Sunny said, which meant something like "This must be where the Quagmires will be hidden."

"I agree with Sunny," Klaus said, "even though there's no description of the item. They don't even write what the letters stand for."

"We'll find out what they stand for," Violet said, "because we're going to find Esmé right this minute, and tell her what's going on. When she finds out, she'll finally believe us about Gunther, and we'll get the Quagmires out of Lot #50 before they leave the city. You were right, Klaus—the time was ripe for your researching skills."

"I guess I was right," Klaus said. "I can

scarcely believe our luck."

The Baudelaires looked again at the page of the catalog, making sure that it was neither a hallucination nor a phantasm. And it wasn't. Right there, written in neat black type under the heading "Lot #50," were three letters, and three punctuation marks, that seemed to spell out the solution to the Baudelaires' problems. The children looked at one another and smiled. All three siblings could scarcely believe their luck. The Baudelaire orphans could scarcely believe that those three letters spelled out the hiding place of the Quagmires as clearly as it spelled out "V.F.D."

C H A P T E R
Ten

"*...and* one of the items in the catalog is listed as 'V.F.D.,' which is the secret that the Quagmires tried to tell us about right before they were kidnapped," Klaus finished.

"This is terrible," Esmé said, and took a sip of the parsley soda she had insisted on pouring for herself before the Baudelaire orphans could tell her everything they had discovered. Then she had insisted on settling herself on the innest couch in her favorite sitting room, and that the three children sit in three chairs grouped around her in a semicircle, before they could relate the story of

Gunther's true identity, the secret passageway behind the sliding elevator doors, the scheme to smuggle the Quagmires out of the city, and the surprising appearance of those three mysterious initials as the description of Lot #50. The three siblings were pleased that their guardian had not dismissed their findings, or argued with them about Gunther or the Quagmires or anything else, but instead had quietly and calmly listened to every detail. In fact, Esmé was so quiet and calm that it was disconcerting, a word which here means "a warning that the Baudelaire children did not heed in time."

"This is the least smashing thing I have ever heard," Esmé said, taking another sip of her in beverage. "Let me see if I have understood everything you have said. Gunther *is* in fact Count Olaf in disguise."

"Yes," Violet said. "His boots are covering up his tattoo, and his monocle makes him scrunch his face up to hide his one eyebrow."

"And he has hidden away the Quagmires in

a cage at the bottom of my elevator shaft," Esmé said, putting her soda glass down on a nearby table.

"Yes," Klaus said. "There's no elevator behind those doors. Somehow Gunther removed it so he could use the shaft as a secret passageway."

"And now he's taken the Quagmires out of the cage," Esmé continued, "and is going to smuggle them out of the city by hiding them inside Lot #50 of the In Auction."

"Kaxret," Sunny said, which meant "You got it, Esmé."

"This is certainly a complicated plot," Esmé said. "I'm surprised that young children such as yourself were able to figure it out, but I'm glad you did." She paused for a moment and removed a speck of dust from one of her fingernails. "And now there's only one thing to do. We'll rush right to Veblen Hall and put a stop to this terrible scheme. We'll have Gunther arrested and the Quagmires set free. We'd better leave right this minute."

Esmé stood up, and beckoned to the children with a faint smile. The children followed her out of the sitting room and past twelve kitchens to the front door, exchanging puzzled glances. Their guardian was right, of course, that they should go to Veblen Hall and expose Gunther and his treachery, but they couldn't help wondering why the city's sixth most important financial advisor was so calm when she said it. The children were so anxious about the Quagmires that they felt as if they were jumping out of their skin, but Esmé led the Baudelaires out of the penthouse as if they were going to the grocery store to purchase whole wheat flour instead of rushing to an auction to stop a horrible crime. As she shut the door of the apartment and turned to smile at the children again, the three siblings could see no sign of anxiousness on her face, and it was disconcerting.

"Klaus and I will take turns carrying you, Sunny," Violet said, lifting her sister up. "That way the trip down the stairs will be easier for you."

"Oh, we don't have to walk down all those stairs," Esmé said.

"That's true," Klaus said. "Sliding down the banisters will be much quicker."

Esmé put one arm around the children and began walking them away from the front door. It was nice to receive an affectionate gesture from their guardian, but her arm was wrapped around them so tightly that they could scarcely move, which was also disconcerting. "We won't have to slide down the banisters, either," she said.

"Then how will we get down from the penthouse?" Violet asked.

Esmé stretched out her other arm, and used one of her long fingernails to press the Up button next to the sliding doors. This was the most disconcerting thing of all, but by now, I'm sorry to say, it was too late. "We'll take the elevator," she said, as the doors slid open, and then with one last smile she swept her arm forward and pushed the Baudelaire orphans into the darkness of the elevator shaft.

Sometimes words are not enough. There are some circumstances so utterly wretched that I cannot describe them in sentences or paragraphs or even a whole series of books, and the terror and woe that the Baudelaire orphans felt after Esmé pushed them into the elevator shaft is one of those most dreadful circumstances that can be represented only with two pages of utter blackness. I have no words for the profound horror the children felt as they tumbled down into the darkness. I can think of no sentence that can convey how loudly they screamed, or how cold the air was as it *whoosh*ed around them while they fell. And there is no paragraph I could possibly type that would enable you to imagine how frightened the Baudelaires were as they plunged toward certain doom.

But I can tell you that they did not die. Not one hair on their heads had been harmed by the time the children finally stopped tumbling through the darkness. They survived the fall from the top of the shaft for the simple reason that they did not reach the bottom. Something broke their fall, a phrase which here means that the Baudelaires' plunge was stopped halfway between the sliding elevator doors and the metal cage where the Quagmires had been locked up. Something broke their fall without even injuring them, and though it at first felt like a miracle, when the children understood that they were alive, and no longer falling, they reached out their hands and soon realized that it felt a lot more like a net. While the Baudelaires were reading the catalog of the In Auction, and telling Esmé what they had learned, someone had stretched a rope net across the entire passageway, and it was this net that had stopped the children from plunging to their doom. Far, far above the orphans was the Squalor penthouse, and far, far below them was the cage in the tiny, filthy room with the hallway leading out of it. The Baudelaire orphans were trapped.

But it is far better to be trapped than to be dead, and the three children hugged each other in relief that something had broken their fall. "Spenset," Sunny said, in a voice hoarse from screaming.

"Yes, Sunny," Violet said, holding her close. "We're alive." She sounded as if she were talking as much to herself as to her sister.

"We're alive," Klaus said, hugging them both. "We're alive, and we're O.K."

"I wouldn't say you were O.K." Esmé's voice called down to them from the top of the passageway. Her voice echoed off the walls of the passageway, but the children could still hear every cruel word. "You're alive, but you're definitely not O.K. As soon as the auction is over and the Quagmires are on their way out of the city, Gunther will come and get you, and I can guarantee that you three orphans will never be O.K. again. What a wonderful and profitable day! My former acting teacher will finally get his hands on not one but two enormous fortunes!"

"Your former acting teacher?" Violet asked in horror. "You mean you've known Gunther's true identity the entire time?"

"Of course I did," Esmé said. "I just had to fool you kids and my dim-witted husband into thinking he was really an auctioneer. Luckily, I am a smashing actress, so it was easy to trick you."

"So you've been working together with that terrible villain?" Klaus called up to her. "How could you do that to us?"

"He's not a terrible villain," Esmé said. "He's a genius! I instructed the doorman not to let you out of the penthouse until Gunther came and retrieved you, but Gunther convinced me that throwing you down there was a better idea, and he was right! Now there's no way you'll make it to the auction and mess up our plans!"

"Zisalem!" Sunny shrieked.

"My sister is right!" Violet cried. "You're our guardian! You're supposed to be keeping us safe, not throwing us down elevator shafts and stealing our fortune!"

"But I want to steal from you," Esmé said.

"I want to steal from you the way Beatrice stole from me."

"What are you talking about?" Klaus asked. "You're already unbelievably wealthy. Why do you want even more money?"

"Because it's in, of course," Esmé said. "Well, toodle-oo, children. 'Toodle-oo' is the in way of saying good-bye to three bratty orphans you're never going to see again."

"*Why?*" Violet cried. "Why are you treating us so terribly?"

Esmé's answer to this question was the cruelest of all, and like a fall down an elevator shaft, there were no words for her reply. She merely laughed, a loud rude cackle that bounced off the walls of the passageway and then faded into silence as their guardian walked away. The Baudelaire orphans looked at one another—or tried to look at one another, in the darkness—and trembled in disgust and fear, shaking the net that had trapped them and saved them at the same time.

"Dielee?" Sunny said miserably, and her siblings knew that she meant "What are we going to do?"

"I don't know," Klaus said, "but we've got to do something."

"And we've got to do it quickly," Violet added, "but this is a very difficult situation. There's no use climbing up or down—the walls feel too smooth."

"And there's no use making a lot of noise to try and get someone's attention," Klaus said. "Even if anybody hears, they'll just think someone is yelling in one of the apartments."

Violet closed her eyes in thought, although it was so dark that it didn't really make a difference if her eyes were closed or open. "Klaus, maybe the time is right for your researching skills," she said after a moment. "Can you think of some moment in history when people got out of a trap like this one?"

"I don't think so," Klaus replied sadly. "In the myth of Hercules, he's trapped between two monsters named Scylla and Charybdis, just like we're trapped between the sliding doors and the floor. But he got out of the trap by turning them into whirlpools."

"Glaucus," Sunny said, which meant something like "But we can't do that."

"I know," Klaus said glumly. "Myths are often entertaining, but they're never very helpful. Maybe the time is ripe for one of Violet's inventions."

"But I don't have any materials to work with," Violet said, reaching out her hand to feel the edges of the net. "I can't use this net for an invention, because if I start to tear it up, we'll fall. The net seems to be attached to the walls with little metal pegs that stick into the walls, but I can't pull those out and use them, either."

"Gyzan?" Sunny asked.

"Yes," Violet replied, "pegs. Feel right here, Sunny. Gunther probably stood on a long ladder to drive these pegs into the walls of the passageway, and then strung the net across the pegs. I guess the walls of the elevator shaft are soft enough that small sharp objects can be stuck into them."

"Tholc?" Sunny asked, which meant "Like teeth?" and instantly her siblings knew what she was thinking.

"No, Sunny," Violet said. "You can't climb up the elevator shaft by using your teeth. It's too dangerous."

"Yoigt," Sunny pointed out, which meant something like "But if I fall, I'll just fall back into the net."

"But what if you get stuck halfway up?" Klaus asked. "Or what if you lose a tooth?"

"Vasta," Sunny said, which meant "I'll just have to risk it—it's our only hope," and her siblings reluctantly agreed. They did not like the idea of their baby sister climbing up to the sliding doors of the ersatz elevator, using only her teeth, but they could think of no other way to escape in time to foil Gunther's plan. The time wasn't ripe for Violet's inventing skills, or for the knowledge Klaus had from his reading, but the time was ripe for Sunny's sharp teeth, and the youngest Baudelaire tilted her head back and then swung forward, sticking one of her teeth into the wall with a rough sound that would make any dentist weep for hours. But the Baudelaires were not dentists, and the three children listened closely in the darkness to hear if Sunny's tooth would stick as firmly as the net pegs. To their delight they heard nothing—no scraping or sliding or cracking or anything that would indicate that Sunny's teeth wouldn't hold. Sunny even shook her head a little bit to see if that would easily dislodge her tooth from the wall, but it remained a firm toothhold. Sunny swung her head slightly, and embedded another tooth, slightly above the first one. The second tooth stuck, so Sunny carefully eased out the first tooth and inserted it once more in the wall, slightly above the second tooth. By spacing her teeth slightly apart, Sunny had moved a few inches up the wall, and by the time she stuck her first tooth above the second one again, her little body was no longer touching the net.

"Good luck, Sunny," Violet said.

"We're rooting for you, Sunny," Klaus said.

Sunny did not reply, but her siblings were not alarmed because they imagined it was difficult to say much when you had a mouthful of wall. So Violet and Klaus merely sat on their net and continued to call up encouragement to their baby sister. Had Sunny been able to climb and speak at the same time, she might have said "Soried," which meant something like "So far so good," or "Yaff," which meant "I think I've reached the halfway point," but the two older Baudelaires heard nothing but the sound of her teeth inserting and detaching themselves in the dark until Sunny triumphantly called down the word "Top!"

"Oh, Sunny!" Klaus cried. "You did it!"

"Way to go!" Violet called up. "Now, go get our makeshift rope from under the bed, and we'll climb up and join you."

"Ganba," Sunny called back, and crawled off. The two older siblings sat and waited in the darkness for a while, marveling at their sister's skills.

"I couldn't have climbed all the way up this passageway," Violet said, "not when I was Sunny's age."

"Me neither," Klaus said, "although we both have regular-sized teeth."

"It's not just the size of her teeth," Violet said, "it's the size of her courage, and the size of her concern for her siblings."

"And the size of the trouble we're in," Klaus added, "and the size of our guardian's treachery. I can't believe Esmé was scheming together with Gunther the entire time. She's as ersatz as her elevator."

"Esmé's a pretty good actress," Violet said comfortingly, "even though she's a terrible person. She had us completely fooled that Gunther had her completely fooled. But what was she talking about when she said—"

"Tada!" Sunny called down from the sliding doors.

"She has the rope," Violet said excitedly. "Tie it to the doorknob, Sunny, using the Devil's Tongue."

"No," Klaus said, "I have a better idea."

"A better idea than climbing out of here?" Violet asked.

"I want to climb out of here," Klaus said, "but I don't think we should climb *up*. Then we'll just be at the penthouse."

"But from the penthouse," Violet said, "we can get to Veblen Hall. We can even slide down the banisters to save time."

"But at the end of the banisters," Klaus said, "is the lobby of the building, and in the lobby is a doorman with strict instructions not to let us leave."

"I hadn't thought about him," Violet said. "He always follows instructions."

"That's why we've got to leave 667 Dark Avenue another way," Klaus said.

"Ditemu," Sunny called down, which meant something like "What other way is there?"

"Down," Klaus said. "That tiny room at the bottom of the elevator shaft has a hallway leading out of it, remember? It's right next to the cage."

"That's true," Violet said. "That must be how Gunther snatched the Quagmires away before we could rescue them. But who knows where it leads?"

"Well, if Gunther took the Quagmires down that hallway," Klaus said, "it must lead to somewhere near Veblen Hall. And that's precisely where we want to go."

"You're right," Violet said. "Sunny, forget about tying the rope to the doorknob. Someone might see it, anyway, and realize we've escaped. Just bring it down here. Do you think you can bite your way back down?"

"Geronimo!" Sunny cried, which meant something like "I don't need to bite my way back down," and the youngest Baudelaire was right. She took a deep breath, and threw herself down the dark passageway, the coil of ersatz rope trailing behind her. This time, the plunge does not need to be represented by pages of darkness, because the terror of the long, dark fall was alleviated—the word "alleviated" here means "not particularly on Sunny's mind"—because the youngest Baudelaire knew that a net, and her siblings, were waiting for her at the bottom. With a *thump!* Sunny landed on the net, and with a slightly smaller *thump!* the coil of rope landed next to her. After making sure her sister was unharmed by the fall, Violet began tying one end of their rope to one of the pegs holding the net in place.

"I'll make sure this end of the rope is secured," Violet said. "Sunny, if your teeth aren't too sore from the climb, use them to cut a hole in the net, so we can climb through it."

"What can I do?" Klaus asked.

"You can pray this works," Violet said, but the Baudelaire sisters were so quick with their tasks that there was no time for even the shortest of religious ceremonies. In a matter of moments, Violet had attached the rope to the peg with some complicated and powerful knots, and Sunny had cut a child-sized hole in the middle of the net. Violet dangled the rope down the hole, and the three children listened until they heard the familiar *clink!* of their ersatz rope against the metal cage. The Baudelaire orphans paused for a moment at the hole in the net, and stared down into the blackness.

"I can't believe we're climbing down this passageway again," Violet said.

"I know what you mean," Klaus said. "If someone had asked me, that day at the beach, if I ever thought we'd be climbing up and down an empty elevator shaft in an attempt to rescue a pair of triplets, I would have said never in a million years. And now we're doing it for the fifth time in twenty-four hours. What happened to us? What led us to this awful place we're staring at now?"

"Misfortune," Violet said quietly.

"A terrible fire," Klaus said.

"Olaf," Sunny said decisively, and began crawling down the rope. Klaus followed his sister down through the hole in the net, and Violet followed Klaus, and the three Baudelaires made the long trek down the bottom half of the passageway until they reached the tiny, filthy room, the empty cage, and the hallway that they hoped would lead them to the In Auction. Sunny squinted up at their rope, making sure that her siblings had safely reached the bottom. Klaus squinted at the hallway, trying to see how long it was, or if there was anybody or anything lurking in it. And Violet squinted in the corner, at the welding torches the children had thrown in the corner when the time had not been ripe to use them.

"We should take these with us," she said.

"But why?" Klaus asked. "They've certainly cooled off long ago."

"They have," Violet said, picking one up.

"And the tips are all bent from throwing them in the corner. But they still might come in handy for something. We don't know what we'll encounter in that hallway, and I don't want to come up shorthanded. Here, Klaus. Here's yours, and here's Sunny's."

The younger Baudelaires took the bent, cooled fire tongs, and then, sticking close to one another, all three children took their first few steps down the hallway. In the utter darkness of this terrible place, the fire tongs seemed like long, slender extensions of the Baudelaires' hands, instead of inventions they were each holding, but this was not what Violet had meant when she said she didn't want them to be shorthanded. "Shorthanded" is a word which here means "unprepared," and Violet was thinking that three children alone in a dark hallway holding fire tongs were perhaps a bit more prepared than three children alone in a dark hallway holding nothing at all. And I'm sorry to tell you that the eldest Baudelaire was absolutely right. The three children couldn't afford to be shorthanded at all, not with the unfair advantage that was lurking at the end of their walk. As they took one cautious step after another, the Baudelaire orphans needed to be as longhanded as possible for the element of surprise that was waiting for them when the dark hallway came to an end.

Eleven

The French expression "cul-de-sac" describes what the Baudelaire orphans found when they reached the end of the dark hallway, and like all French expressions, it is most easily understood when you translate each French word into English. The word "de," for instance, is a very common French word, so even if I didn't know a word of French, I would be certain that "de" means "of." The word "sac" is less common, but I am fairly certain that it means something like "mysterious circumstances." And the word "cul" is such a rare French word that I am forced

to guess at its translation, and my guess is that in this case it would mean "At the end of the dark hallway, the Baudelaire children found an assortment," so that the expression "cul-de-sac" here means "At the end of the dark hallway, the Baudelaire children found an assortment of mysterious circumstances."

If the Baudelaires had been able to choose a French expression that would be waiting for them at the end of the hallway, they might have chosen one that meant "By the time the three children rounded the last dark corner of the corridor, the police had captured Gunther and rescued the Quagmire triplets," or at least "The Baudelaires were delighted to see that the hallway led straight to Veblen Hall, where the In Auction was taking place." But the end of the hallway proved to be as mysterious and worrisome as the rest of it. The entire length of the hallway was very dark, and it had so many twists and turns that the three children frequently found themselves bumping into the walls. The ceiling of the hallway was very low—Gunther must have had to crouch when he used it for his treacherous plans—and over their heads the three children could hear a variety of noises that told them where the hallway was probably taking them. After the first few curves, they heard the muted voice of the doorman, and his footsteps as he walked overhead, and the Baudelaires realized that they must be underneath the lobby of the Squalors' apartment building. After a few more curves, they heard two men discussing ocean decorations, and they realized they must be walking beneath Dark Avenue. And after a few more curves, they heard the rickety rattle of an old trolley that was passing over their heads, and the children knew that the hallway was leading them underneath one of the city's trolley stations. On and on the hallway curved, and the Baudelaires heard a variety of city sounds—the clopping of horses' hooves, the grinding of factory equipment, the tolling of church bells and the clatter of people dropping things—but when they finally reached the corridor's end, there was no sound over their heads at all. The Baudelaires stood still and tried to imagine a place in the city where it was absolutely silent.

"Where do you think we are?" Violet asked, straining her ears to listen even more closely. "It's as silent as a tomb up there."

"That's not what I'm worried about," Klaus answered, poking the wall with his fire tong. "I can't find which way the hallway curves. I think we might be at a dead end."

"A dead end!" Violet said, and poked the opposite wall with her tong. "It can't be a dead end. Nobody builds a hallway that goes no-where."

"Pratjic," Sunny said, which meant "Gunther must have ended up somewhere if he took this passageway."

"I'm poking every inch of these walls," Klaus said grimly, "and there's no door or stair-way or curve or anything. It's a dead end, all right. There's no other word for it. Actually, there's a French expression for 'dead end,' but I can't remember what is."

"I guess we have to retrace our steps," Violet said miserably. "I guess we have to turn around, and make our way back down the corridor, and climb up to the net, and have Sunny teeth her way to the penthouse and find some more materials to make an ersatz rope, and climb all the way up to the top floor, and slide down the banisters to the lobby, and sneak past the doorman and run to Veblen Hall."

"Pyetian," Sunny said, which meant something like "We'll never make it there in time to expose Gunther and save the Quagmires."

"I know," Violet sighed. "But I don't know what else we can do. It looks like we're short-handed, even with these tongs."

"If we had some shovels," Klaus said, "we could try to dig our way out of the hallway, but we can't use the tongs as shovels."

"Tenti," Sunny said, which meant "If we

had some dynamite, we could blast our way out of the hallway, but we can't use the tongs as dynamite."

"But we might be able to use them as noise-makers," Violet said suddenly. "Let's bang on the ceiling with our tongs, and see if we can attract the attention of someone who is passing by."

"It doesn't sound like anyone is passing by," Klaus said, "but it's worth a try. Here, Sunny, I'll pick you up so your tong can reach the ceiling, too."

Klaus picked his sister up, and the three children began to bang on the ceiling, planning to make a racket that would last for several minutes. But as soon as the their tongs first hit the ceiling, the Baudelaires were showered with black dust. It rained down on them like a dry, filthy storm, and the children had to cut short their banging to cough and rub their eyes and spit out the dust that had fallen into their mouths.

"Ugh!" Violet spat. "This tastes terrible."

"It tastes like burned toast," Klaus said.

"Peflob!" Sunny shrieked.

At that, Violet stopped coughing, and licked the tip of her finger in thought. "It's ashes," she said. "Maybe we're below a fireplace."

"I don't think so," Klaus said. "Look up."

The Baudelaires looked up, and saw that the black dust had uncovered a very small stripe of light, barely as wide as a pencil. The children gazed up into it, and could see the morning sun gazing right back at them.

"Tisdu?" Sunny said, which meant "Where in the city can you find ashes outdoors?"

"Maybe we're below a barbeque pit," Klaus said.

"Well, we'll find out soon enough," Violet replied, and began to sweep more dust away from the ceiling. As it fell on the children in a thick, dark cloud, the skinny stripe of light became four skinny stripes, like a drawing of a square on the ceiling. By the light of the square, the Baudelaires could see a pair of hinges. "Look," Violet said, "it's a trapdoor. We couldn't see it in the darkness of the hallway, but there it is."

Klaus pressed his tong against the trapdoor to try to open it, but it didn't budge. "It's locked, of course," he said. "I bet Gunther locked it behind him when he took the Quagmires away."

Violet looked up at the trapdoor, and the other children could see, by the light of the sun streaming in, that she was tying her hair up in a ribbon to keep it out of her eyes. "A lock isn't going to stop us," she said. "Not when we've come all this way. I think the time is finally ripe for these tongs—not as welding torches, and not as noisemakers." She smiled, and turned her attention to her siblings. "We can use them as crowbars," she said excitedly.

"Herdiset?" Sunny asked.

"A crowbar is a sort of portable lever," Violet said, "and these tongs will work perfectly. We'll stick the bent end into the part where the light is shining through, and then push the rest of the tong sharply down. It should bring the trapdoor down with it. Understand?"

"I think so," Klaus said. "Let's try."

The Baudelaires tried. Carefully, they stuck the part of the tongs that had been heated in the oven into one side of the square of light. And then, grunting with the effort, they pushed the straight end of the tongs down as sharply as they could, and I'm happy to report that the crowbars worked perfectly. With a tremendous crackling sound and another cloud of ashes, the trapdoor bent on its hinges and opened toward the children, who had to duck as it swung over their heads. Sunlight streamed into the hallway, and the Baudelaires saw that they had finally come to the end of their long, dark journey.

"It worked!" Violet cried. "It really worked!"

"The time was ripe for your inventing skills!" Klaus cried. "The solution was right on the tip of our tongs!"

"Up!" Sunny shrieked, and the children agreed. By standing on tiptoe, the Baudelaires could grab ahold of the hinges and pull themselves out of the hallway, leaving behind their crowbars, and in a moment the three children were squinting in the sunlight.

One of my most prized possessions is a small wooden box with a special lock on it that is more than five hundred years old and works according to a secret code that my grandfather taught me. My grandfather learned it from his grandfather, and his grandfather learned it from his grandfather, and I would teach it to my grandchild if I thought that I would ever have a family of my own instead of living out the remainder of my days all alone in this world. The small wooden box is one of my most prized possessions, because when the lock is opened according to the code, a small silver key may be found inside, and this key fits the lock on one of my other most prized possessions, which is a slightly larger wooden box given to me by a woman whom my grandfather always refused to speak about. Inside this slightly larger wooden box is a roll of parchment, a word which here means "some very old paper printed with a map of the city at the time when the Baudelaire orphans lived in it." The map has every single detail of the city written down in dark blue ink, with measurements of buildings and sketches of costumes and charts of changes in the weather all added in the margins by the map's twelve previous owners, all of whom are now dead. I have spent more hours than I can ever count going over every inch of this map as carefully as possible, so that everything that can be learned from it can be copied into my files and then into books such as this one, in the hopes that the general public will finally learn every detail of the treacherous conspiracy I have spent my life trying to escape. The map contains thousands of fascinating things that have been discovered by all sorts of explorers, criminal investigators, and circus performers over the years, but the most fascinating thing that the map contains was discovered just at this moment by the three Baudelaire children. Sometimes, in the dead of night when I cannot sleep, I rise from my bed and work the code on the small wooden box to retrieve the silver key that opens the slightly larger wooden box so I can sit at my desk and look once again, by candlelight, at the two dotted lines indicating the underground hallway that begins at the bottom of the elevator shaft at 667 Dark Avenue and ends at the trapdoor that the Baudelaires managed to open with their ersatz crowbars. I stare and stare at the part of the city where the orphans climbed out of that ghastly corridor, but no matter how much I stare I can scarcely believe my own eyes, any more than the youngsters could believe theirs.

The siblings had been in darkness for so long that their eyes took a long time to get used to properly lit surroundings, and they stood for a moment, rubbing their eyes and trying to see exactly where the trapdoor had led them. But in the sudden brightness of the morning sun, the only thing the children could see was the chubby shadow of a man standing near them.

"Excuse me," Violet called, while her eyes were still adjusting. "We need to get to Veblen Hall. It's an emergency. Could you tell me where it is?"

"Ju-just two blo-blocks that way," the shadow stuttered, and the children gradually realized that it was a slightly overweight mail-man, pointing down the street and looking at the children fearfully. "Please don't hurt me," the mailman added, stepping away from the youngsters.

"We're not going to hurt you," Klaus said, wiping ashes off his glasses.

"Ghosts always say that," the mailman said, "but then they hurt you anyway."

"But we're not ghosts," Violet said.

"Don't tell me you're not ghosts," the mail-man replied. "I saw you rise out of the ashes myself, as if you had come from the center of the earth. People have always said it's haunted here on the empty lot where the Baudelaire mansion burned down, and now I know it's true."

The mailman ran away before the Baudelaires could reply, but the three children were too amazed by his words to speak to him anyway. They blinked and blinked in the morning sun, and finally their eyes adjusted enough to see that the mailman was right. It was true. It was not true that the three children were ghosts, of course. They were not spooky creatures who had risen from the center of the earth, but three orphans who had hoisted themselves out of the hallway. But the mailman had spoken the truth when he had told them where they were. The Baudelaire orphans looked around them, and huddled together as if they were still in a dark hallway instead of outdoors in broad daylight, standing amid the ashy ruins of their destroyed home.

Several years before the Baudelaires were born, Veblen Hall won the prestigious Door Prize, an award given each year to the city's best-constructed opening, and if you ever find yourself standing in front of Veblen Hall, as the Baudelaire orphans did that morning, you will immediately see why the committee awarded the shiny pink trophy to the door's polished wooden planks, its exquisite brass hinges and its gorgeous, shiny doorknob, fashioned out of the world's second-finest crystal. But the three siblings were in no state to appreciate architectural detail. Violet led the way up the stairs to Veblen Hall and grabbed the doorknob without a thought to the ashy smear she would leave on its polished surface. If I had been with the Baudelaires, I never would have opened the award-winning door. I would have considered myself lucky to have gotten out of the net suspended in the middle of the elevator shaft, and to have escaped Gunther's evil plan, and I would have fled to some remote corner of the world and hid from Gunther and his associates for the rest of my life rather than risk another encounter with this treacherous villain—an encounter, I'm sorry to say, that will only bring more misery into the three orphans' lives. But these three children were far more courageous than I shall ever be, and they paused just for a moment to gather all of this courage up and use it.

"Beyond this doorknob," Violet said, "is our last chance at revealing Gunther's true identity and his terrible plans."

"Just past those brass hinges," Klaus said, "is our final opportunity to save the Quagmires from being smuggled out of the country."

"Sorusu," Sunny said, which meant "Behind those wooden planks lies the answer to the mystery of V.F.D., and why the secret hallway led us to the place where the Baudelaire mansion burned to the ground, killing our parents, and beginning the series of unfortunate events that haunt us wherever we go."

The Baudelaires looked at one another and stood up as straight as they could, as if their backbones were as strong as their courage, and Violet opened the door of Veblen Hall; and instantly the orphans found themselves in the middle of a hubbub, a word which here means "a huge crowd of people in an enormous, fancy room." Veblen Hall had a very high ceiling, a very shiny floor, and one massive window that had won first runner-up for the Window Prize the previous year. Hanging from the ceiling were three huge banners, one with the word "In" written on it, one with the word "Auction" written on it, and one last one, twice as big as the others, with a huge portrait of Gunther. Standing on the floor were at least two hundred people, and the Baudelaires could tell that it was a very in crowd. Almost everyone was wearing pinstripe suits, sipping tall frosty glasses of parsley soda, and eating salmon puffs offered by some costumed waiters from Café Salmonella, which had apparently been hired to cater the auction. The Baudelaires were in regular clothes rather than pinstripes, and they were covered in dirt from the tiny, filthy room at the bottom of the elevator shaft, and in ashes from the Baudelaire lot where the hallway had led them. The in crowd would have frowned upon such attire had they noticed the children, but everyone was too busy gazing at the far end of the room to turn around and see who had walked through the award-winning door.

For at the far end of Veblen Hall, underneath the biggest banner and in front of the massive window, Gunther was standing up on a small stage and speaking into a microphone. On one side of him was a small glass vase with blue flowers painted on it, and on the other was Esmé, who was sitting in a fancy chair and gazing at Gunther as if he were the cat's pajamas, a phrase which here means "a charming and handsome gentleman instead of a cruel and dishonest villain."

"Lot #46, please," Gunther was saying into the microphone. With all of their exploration of dark passageways, the Baudelaires had almost forgotten that Gunther was pretending that he wasn't fluent in English. "Please, gentlemen and ladies, see the vase with blue flowers. Vases in. Glass in. Flowers in, please, especially the flowers that are blue. Who bid?"

"One hundred," called out a voice from the crowd.

"One hundred fifty," another voice said.

"Two hundred," another said.

"Two hundred fifty," returned the person who had bid first.

"Two hundred fifty-three," another said.

"We're just in time," Klaus whispered to Violet. "V.F.D. is Lot #50. Do we wait to speak up until then, or do we confront Gunther right now?"

"I don't know," Violet whispered back. "We were so focused on getting to Veblen Hall in time that we forgot to think up a plan of action."

"Is two hundred fifty-three last bidding of people, please?" Gunther asked, into the microphone. "O.K. Here is vase, please. Give money, please, to Mrs. Squalor." A pinstriped woman walked to the edge of the stage and handed a stack of bills to Esmé, who smiled greedily and handed her the vase in exchange. Watching Esmé count the pile of bills and then calmly place them in her pinstripe purse, while somewhere backstage the Quagmires were trapped inside whatever V.F.D. was, made the Baudelaires feel sick to their stomachs.

"Evomer," Sunny said, which meant "I can't stand it any longer. Let's tell everyone in this room what is really going on."

"Excuse me," said somebody, and the three children looked up to see a stern-looking man peering down at them from behind some very large sunglasses. He was holding a salmon puff in one hand and pointing at the Baudelaires with the other. "I'm going to have to ask you to leave Veblen Hall at once," he said. "This is the In Auction. It's no place for grimy little children like yourselves."

"But we're supposed to be here," Violet said, thinking quickly. "We're meeting our guardians."

"Don't make me laugh," the man said, although it looked like he had never laughed in his life. "What sort of people would be caring for such dirty little kids?"

"Jerome and Esmé Squalor," Klaus said. "We've been living in their penthouse."

"We'll see about this," the man said. "Jerry, get over here!"

At the sound of the man's raised voice, a few people turned around and looked at the children, but almost everyone kept listening to Gunther as he began to auction off Lot #47, which he explained was a pair of ballet slippers, please, made of chocolate. Jerome detached himself from a small circle of people and walked over to the stern man to see what the matter was. When he caught sight of the orphans, he looked as if you could have knocked him over with a feather, a phrase which here means he seemed happy but extremely surprised to see them.

"I'm very happy to see you," he said, "but extremely surprised. Esmé told me you weren't feeling very well."

"So you know these children, Jerome?" the man in sunglasses said.

"Of course I know them," Jerome replied. "They're the Baudelaires. I was just telling you about them."

"Oh yes," the man said, losing interest. "Well, if they're orphans, then I guess it's O.K. for them to be here. But Jerry, you've got to buy them some new clothes!"

The man walked away before Jerome could reply. "I don't like to be called Jerry," he admitted to the children, "but I don't like to argue with him, either. Well, Baudelaires, are you feeling better?"

The children stood for a moment and looked up at their guardian. They noticed that he had a half-eaten salmon puff in his hand, even though he had told the siblings that he didn't like salmon. Jerome had probably not wanted to argue with the waiters in the salmon costumes, either. The Baudelaires looked at him, and then looked at one another. They did not feel better at all. They knew that Jerome would not want to argue with them if they told him once more about Gunther's true identity. He would not want to argue with Esmé if they told him about her part in the treacherous scheme. And he would not want to argue with Gunther if they told him that the Quagmires were trapped inside one of the items at the In Auction. The Baudelaires did not feel better at all as they realized that the only person who could help them was someone who could be knocked over with a feather.

"Menrov?" Sunny said.

"Menrov?" Jerome repeated, smiling down at the littlest Baudelaire. "What does 'Menrov?' mean?"

"I'll tell you what it means," Klaus said, thinking quickly. Perhaps there was a way to have Jerome help them, without making him argue with anyone. "It means 'Would you do us a favor, Jerome?'"

Violet and Sunny looked at their brother curiously. "Menrov?" didn't mean "Would you do us a favor, Jerome?" and Klaus most certainly knew it. "Menrov?" meant something more like "Should we try to tell Jerome about Gunther and Esmé and the Quagmire triplets?" but the sisters kept quiet, knowing that Klaus must have a good reason to lie to his guardian.

"Of course I'll do you a favor," Jerome said. "What is it?"

"My sisters and I would really like to own one of the lots at this auction," Klaus said. "We were wondering if you might buy it for us, as a gift."

"I suppose so," Jerome said. "I didn't know you three were interested in in items."

"Oh, yes," Violet said, understanding at once what Klaus was up to. "We're very anxious to own Lot #50—V.F.D."

"V.F.D.?" Jerome asked. "What does that stand for?"

"It's a surprise," Klaus said quickly. "Would you bid for it?"

"If it's very important to you," Jerome said, "I suppose I will, but I don't want you to get spoiled. You certainly arrived in time. It looks like Gunther is just finishing the bidding on those ballet shoes, so we're coming right up to Lot #50. Let's go watch the auction from where I was standing. There's an excellent view of the stage, and there's a friend of yours standing with me."

"A friend of ours?" Violet asked.

"You'll see," Jerome said, and they did see. When they followed Jerome across the enormous room to watch the auction underneath the "In" banner, they found Mr. Poe, holding a glass of parsley soda and coughing into his white handkerchief.

"You could knock me over with a feather," Mr. Poe said, when he was done coughing. "What are you Baudelaires doing here?"

"What are *you* doing here?" Klaus asked. "You told us you would be on a helicopter ride to a mountain peak."

Mr. Poe paused to cough into his white handkerchief again. "The reports about the mountain peak turned out to be false," Mr. Poe said, when the coughing fit had passed. "I now know for certain that the Quagmire twins are being forced to work at a glue factory nearby. I'm heading over there later, but I wanted to stop by the In Auction. Now that I'm Vice President in Charge of Orphan Affairs, I'm making more money, and my wife wanted to see if I could buy a bit of ocean decoration."

"But—" Violet started to say, but Mr. Poe shushed her.

"Shush," he said. "Gunther is beginning Lot #48, and that's what I want to bid on."

"Please, Lot #48," Gunther announced. His shiny eyes regarded the crowd from behind his monocle, but he did not appear to spot the Baudelaires. "Is large statue of fish, painted red, please. Very big, very in. Big enough to sleep inside this fish, if you are in the mood, please. Who bid?"

"I bid, Gunther," Mr. Poe called out. "One hundred."

"Two hundred," called out another voice from the crowd.

Klaus leaned in close to Mr. Poe to talk to him without Jerome hearing. "Mr. Poe, there's something you should know about Gunther," he said, thinking that if he could convince Mr. Poe, then the Baudelaires wouldn't have to continue

their charade, a word which here means "pretending to want V.F.D. so Jerome would bid on
it and save the Quagmires without knowing it."
"He's really—"

"An in auctioneer, I know," Mr. Poe finished
for him, and bid again. "Two hundred six."

"Three hundred," replied the other voice.

"No, no," Violet said. "He's not really an
auctioneer at all. He's Count Olaf in disguise."

"Three hundred twelve," Mr. Poe called
out, and then frowned down at the children.
"Don't be ridiculous," he said to them. "Count
Olaf is a criminal. Gunther is just a foreigner.
I can't remember the word for a fear of for-
eigners, but I am surprised that you children
have such a fear."

"Four hundred," called out the other voice.

"The word is 'xenophobia,'" Klaus said,
"but it doesn't apply here, because Gunther's
not really a foreigner. He's not even really
Gunther!"

Mr. Poe took out his handkerchief again,

and the Baudelaires waited as he coughed into it before replying. "You're not making any sense," he said finally. "Can we please discuss this after I buy this ocean decoration? I bid four hundred nine!"

"Five hundred," called out the other voice.

"I give up," Mr. Poe said, and coughed into his handkerchief. "Five hundred is too much to pay for a big herring statue."

"Five hundred is highest bid, please," Gunther said, and smiled at someone in the crowd. "Please will the winner give money to Mrs. Squalor, please."

"Why, look, children," Jerome said. "The doorman bought that big red fish."

"The doorman?" Mr. Poe said, as the doorman handed Esmé a sack of coins and, with difficulty, lifted the enormous red fish statue off the stage, his hands still hidden in his long, long sleeves. "I'm surprised that a doorman can afford to buy anything at the In Auction."

"He told me once he was an actor, too,"

Jerome said. "He's an interesting fellow. Care to meet him?"

"That's very nice of you," Mr. Poe said, and coughed into his handkerchief. "I'm certainly meeting all sorts of interesting people since my promotion."

The doorman was struggling past the children with his scarlet herring when Jerome tapped him on the shoulder. "Come meet Mr. Poe," he said.

"I don't have time to meet anyone," the doorman replied. "I have to get this in the boss's truck and—" The doorman stopped midsentence when he caught sight of the Baudelaire children. "You're not supposed to be here!" he said. "You're not supposed to have left the penthouse."

"Oh, but they're feeling better now," Jerome said, but the doorman wasn't listening. He had turned around—swatting several pinstripe members of the crowd with his fish statue as he did so—and was calling up to the people on the stage. "Hey, boss!" he said, and both Esmé and Gunther turned to look as he pointed at the three Baudelaires. "The orphans are here!"

Esmé gasped, and she was so affected by the element of surprise that she almost dropped her sack of coins, but Gunther merely turned his head and looked directly at the children. His eyes shone very, very brightly, even the one behind his monocle, and the Baudelaires were horrified to recognize his expression. Gunther was smiling as if he had just told a joke, and it was an expression he wore when his treacherous mind was working its hardest.

"Orphans in," he said, still insisting on pretending that he could not speak English properly. "O.K. for orphans to be here, please." Esmé looked curiously at Gunther, but then shrugged, and gestured to the doorman with a long-nailed hand that everything was O.K. The doorman shrugged back at her, and then gave the Baudelaires a strange smile and walked out of the award-winning door. "We will skip Lot #49, please," Gunther continued. "We will bid on Lot #50, please, and then, please, auction is over."

"But what about all the other items?" some-one called.

"Skip 'em," Esmé said dismissively. "I've made enough money today."

"I never thought I'd hear Esmé say that," Jerome murmured.

"Lot #50, please," Gunther announced, and pushed an enormous cardboard box onto the stage. It was as big as the fish statue—just the right size for storing two small children. The box had "V.F.D." printed on it in big black let-ters, and the Baudelaires saw that some tiny airholes had been poked in the top. The three siblings could picture their friends, trapped inside the box and terrified that they were about to be smuggled out of the city. "V.F.D. please," Gunther said. "Who bid?"

"I bid twenty," Jerome said, and winked at the children.

"What in the world is 'V.F.D.'?" Mr. Poe asked.

Violet knew that she had no time to try to explain everything to Mr. Poe. "It's a surprise," she said. "Stick around and find out."

"Fifty," said another voice, and the Baudelaires turned to see that this second bid had come from the man in sunglasses who had asked them to leave.

"That doesn't look like one of Gunther's assistants," Klaus whispered to his sisters.

"You never know," Violet replied. "They're hard to spot."

"Fifty-five," Jerome called out. Esmé frowned at him, and then gave the Baudelaires a very mean glare.

"One hundred," the man in sunglasses said.

"Goodness, children," Jerome said. "This is getting very expensive. Are you sure you want this V.F.D.?"

"You're buying this for the children?" Mr.

Poe said. "Please, Mr. Squalor, don't spoil these youngsters."

"He's not spoiling us!" Violet said, afraid that Gunther would stop the bidding. "Please, Jerome, *please* buy Lot #50 for us. We'll explain everything later."

Jerome sighed. "Very well," he said. "I guess it's only natural that you'd want some in things, after spending time with Esmé. I bid one hundred eight."

"Two hundred," the man in sunglasses said. The Baudelaires craned their necks to try and get a better look at him, but the man in sunglasses didn't look any more familiar.

"Two hundred four," Jerome said, and then looked down at the children. "I won't bid any higher, children. This is getting much too expensive, and bidding is too much like arguing for me to enjoy it."

"Three hundred," the man in sunglasses said, and the Baudelaire children looked at one another in horror. What could they do? Their friends were about to slip out of their grasp.

"Please, Jerome," Violet said. "I beg of you, *please* buy this for us."

Jerome shook his head. "Someday you'll understand," he said. "It's not worth it to spend money on silly in things."

Klaus turned to Mr. Poe. "Mr. Poe," he said, "would you be willing to loan us some money from the bank?"

"To buy a cardboard box?" Mr. Poe said. "I should say not. Ocean decorations are one thing, but I don't want you children wasting money on a box of something, no matter what it is."

"Final bid is three hundred, please," Gunther said, turning and giving Esmé a monocled wink. "Please, sir, if—"

"Thousand!"

Gunther stopped at the sound of a new bidder for Lot #50. Esmé's eyes widened, and she grinned at the thought of putting such an enormous sum in her pinstripe purse. The in crowd looked around, trying to figure out where this new voice was coming from, but nobody suspected such a long and valuable word would originate in the mouth of a tiny baby who was no bigger than a salami.

"Thousand!" Sunny shrieked again, and her siblings held their breath. They knew, of course, that their sister had no such sum of money, but they hoped that Gunther could not see where this bid was coming from, and would be too greedy to find out. The ersatz auctioneer looked at Esmé, and then again out into the crowd.

"Where in the world did Sunny get that kind of money?" Jerome asked Mr. Poe.

"Well, when the children were in boarding school," Mr. Poe answered, "Sunny worked as a receptionist, but I had no idea that her salary was that high."

"Thousand!" Sunny insisted, and finally Gunther gave in.

"The highest bid is now one thousand," he said, and then remembered to pretend that he wasn't fluent in English. "Please," he added.

"Good grief!" the man in sunglasses said. "I'm not going to pay more than one thousand for V.F.D. It's not worth it."

"It is to us," Violet said fiercely, and the three children walked toward the stage. Every eye in the crowd fell on the siblings as they left an ashy trail behind them on their way to the cardboard box. Jerome looked confused. Mr. Poe looked befuddled, a word which here means "as confused as Jerome." Esmé looked vicious. The man in sunglasses looked like he had lost an auction. And Gunther kept smiling, as if a joke he had told was only getting funnier and funnier. Violet and Klaus climbed up on the stage and then hoisted Sunny up alongside them, and the three orphans looked fiercely at the terrible man who had imprisoned their friends.

"Give your thousand, please, to Mrs. Squalor," Gunther said, grinning down at the children. "And then auction is over."

"The only thing that is over," Klaus said, "is your horrible plan."

"Silko!" Sunny agreed, and then, using her teeth even though they were still sore from climbing up the elevator shaft, the youngest Baudelaire bit into the cardboard box and began ripping it apart, hoping that she wasn't hurting Duncan and Isadora Quagmire as she did so.

"Wait a minute, kids!" Esmé snarled, getting out of her fancy chair and stomping over to the box. "You can't open the box until you give me the money. That's illegal!"

"What is illegal," Klaus said, "is auctioning off children. And soon this whole room will see that you have broken the law!"

"What's this?" Mr. Poe asked, striding toward the stage. Jerome followed him, looking from the orphans to his wife in confusion.

"The Quagmire triplets are in this box," Violet explained, helping her sister tear it open. "Gunther and Esmé are trying to smuggle them out of the country."

"What?" Jerome cried. "Esmé, is this true?"

Esmé did not reply, but in a moment everyone would see if it was true or not. The children had torn away a large section of the cardboard, and they could see a layer of white paper inside, as if Gunther had wrapped up the Quagmires the way you might have the butcher wrap up a pair of chicken breasts.

"Hang on, Duncan!" Violet called, into the paper. "Just a few more seconds, Isadora! We're getting you out of there!"

Mr. Poe frowned, and coughed into his white handkerchief. "Now look here, Baudelaires," he said sternly, when his coughing spell was over, "I have reliable information that the Quagmires are in a glue factory, not inside a cardboard box."

"We'll see about that," Klaus said, and Sunny gave the box another big bite. With a loud shredding sound it split right down the middle, and the contents of the box spilled out all over the stage. It is necessary to use the expression "a red herring" to describe what was inside the cardboard box. A red herring, of course, is a type of fish, but it is also an expression that means "a distracting and misleading clue." Gunther had used the initials V.F.D. on the box to mislead the Baudelaires into thinking that their friends were trapped inside, and I'm sorry to tell you that the Baudelaires did not realize it was a red herring until they looked around the stage and saw what the box contained.

CHAPTER Thirteen

"*These* are *doilies*," Violet cried. "This box is full of *doilies*!" And it was true. Scattered around the stage, spilling out of the remains of the cardboard box, were hundreds and hundreds of small, round napkins with a strip of lace around them—the sort of napkins that you might use to decorate a plate of cookies at a fancy tea party.

"Of course," the man in sunglasses said. He approached the stage and removed his sunglasses, and the Baudelaires could see that he wasn't one of Gunther's associates after all. He was just a bidder, in a pinstripe suit. "I was going to give them to my brother for a birthday present. They're Very Fancy Doilies. What else could V.F.D. stand for?"

"Yes," Gunther said, smiling at the children. "What else could it stand for, please?"

"I don't know," Violet said, "but the Quagmires didn't find out a secret about fancy napkins. Where have you put them, Olaf?"

"What is Olaf, please?" Gunther asked.

"Now, Violet," Jerome said. "We agreed that we wouldn't argue about Gunther anymore. Please excuse these children, Gunther. I think they must be ill."

"We're not ill!" Klaus cried. "We've been tricked! This box of doilies was a red herring!"

"But the red herring was Lot #48," someone in the crowd said.

"Children, I'm very disturbed by your behavior," Mr. Poe said. "You look like you haven't washed in a week. You're spending your money on ridiculous items. You run around accusing everybody of being Count Olaf in disguise. And now you've made a big mess of doilies on the floor. Someone is likely to trip and fall on all these slippery napkins. I would have thought that the Squalors would be raising you better than this."

"Well, we're not going to raise them anymore," Esmé said. "Not after they've made such a spectacle of themselves. Mr. Poe, I want these terrible children placed out of my care. It's not worth it to have orphans, even if they're in."

"Esmé!" Jerome cried. "They lost their parents! Where else can they go?"

"Don't argue with me," Esmé snapped, "and I'll tell you where they can go. They can—"

"With me, please," Gunther said, and placed one of his scraggly hands on Violet's shoulder. Violet remembered when this treacherous villain had plotted to marry her, and shuddered underneath his greedy fingers. "I am loving of the children. I would be happy, please, to raise three children of my own." He put his other scraggly hand on Klaus's shoulder, and then stepped forward as if he was going to put one of his boots on Sunny's shoulder so all three Baudelaires would be locked in a sinister embrace. But Gunther's foot did not land on Sunny's shoulder. It landed on a doily, and in a second Mr. Poe's prediction that someone would trip and fall came true. With a papery *thump!* Gunther was suddenly on the ground, his arms flailing wildly in the doilies and his legs flailing madly on the floor of the stage. "Please!" he shouted as he hit the ground, but his wiggling limbs only made him slip more, and the doilies began to spread out across the stage and fall to the floor of Veblen Hall. The Baudelaires watched the fancy napkins flutter around them, making flimsy, whispering sounds as they fell, but then they heard two weighty sounds, one after the other, as if Gunther's fall had made something heavier fall to the floor, and when they turned their heads to follow the sound, they saw Gunther's boots lying on the floor, one at Jerome's feet and one at Mr. Poe's.

"Please!" Gunther shouted again, as he struggled to stand up, but when he finally got to his feet, everyone else in the room was looking at them.

"Look!" the man who had been wearing sunglasses said. "The auctioneer wasn't wearing any socks! That's not very polite!"

"And look!" someone else said. "He has a doily stuck between two of his toes! That's not very comfortable!"

"And look!" Jerome said. "He has a tattoo of an eye on his ankle! He's not Gunther!"

"He's not an auctioneer!" Mr. Poe cried. "He's not even a foreigner! He's Count Olaf!"

"He's more than Count Olaf," Esmé said, walking slowly toward the terrible villain. "He's a genius! He's a wonderful acting teacher! And he's the handsomest, innest man in town!"

"Don't be absurd!" Jerome said. "Ruthless kidnapping villains aren't in!"

"You're right," said Count Olaf, and what a relief it is to call him by his proper name. Olaf tossed away his monocle and put his arm around Esmé. "We're not in. We're out—out of the city! Come on, Esmé!"

With a shriek of laughter, Olaf took Esmé's hand and leaped from the stage, elbowing aside the in crowd as he began running toward the exit.

"They're escaping!" Violet cried, and jumped off the stage to chase after them. Klaus and Sunny followed her as fast as their legs could carry them, but Olaf and Esmé had longer legs, which in this case was just as unfair an advantage as the element of surprise. By the time the Baudelaires had run to the banner with Gunther's face on it, Olaf and Esmé had reached the banner with "Auction" printed on it, and by the time the children reached that banner, the two villains had run past the "In" banner and through the award-winning door of Veblen Hall.

"Egad!" Mr. Poe cried. "We can't let that dreadful man escape for the sixth time! After him, everyone! That man is wanted for a wide variety of violent and financial crimes!"

The in crowd sprang into action, and began chasing after Olaf and Esmé, and you may choose to believe, as this story nears its conclusion, that with so many people chasing after this wretched villain, it would be impossible for him to escape. You may wish to close this book without finishing it, and imagine that Olaf and Esmé were captured, and that the Quagmire triplets were rescued, and that the true meaning of V.F.D. was discovered and that the mystery of the secret hallway to the ruined Baudelaire mansion was solved and that everyone held a delightful picnic to celebrate all this good fortune and that there were enough ice cream sandwiches to go around. I certainly wouldn't blame you for imagining these things, because I imagine them all the time. Late at night, when not even the map of the city can comfort me, I close my eyes and imagine all those happy comforting things surrounding the Baudelaire children, instead of all those doilies that surrounded them and brought yet another scoop of misfortune into their lives. Because when Count Olaf and Esmé Squalor flung open the door of Veblen Hall, they let in an afternoon breeze that made all the very fancy doilies flutter over the Baudelaires' heads and then settle back down on the floor behind them, and in one slippery moment the entire in crowd was falling all over one another in a papery, pinstripe blur. Mr. Poe fell on Jerome. Jerome fell on the man who had been wearing sunglasses, and his sunglasses fell on the woman who had bid highest on Lot #47. That woman dropped her chocolate ballet slippers, and those slippers fell on Count Olaf's boots, and those boots fell on three more doilies that made four more people slip and fall on one another and soon the entire crowd was in a hopeless tangle.

But the Baudelaires did not even glance

back to see the latest grief that the doilies had caused. They kept their eyes on the pair of loathsome people who were running down the steps of Veblen Hall toward a big black pickup truck. Behind the wheel of the pickup truck was the doorman, who had finally done the sensible thing and rolled up his oversized sleeves, but that must have been a difficult task, for as the children gazed into the truck they caught a glimpse of two hooks where the doorman's hands should have been.

"The hook-handed man!" Klaus cried. "He was right under our noses the entire time!"

Count Olaf turned to sneer at the children just as he reached the pickup truck. "He might have been right under your noses," he snarled, "but soon he will be at your throats. I'll be back, Baudelaires! Soon the Quagmire sapphires will be mine, but I haven't forgotten about your fortune!"

"Gonope?" Sunny shrieked, and Violet was quick to translate.

"Where are Duncan and Isadora?" she said. "Where have you taken them?"

Olaf and Esmé looked at one another, and burst into laughter as they slipped into the black truck. Esmé jerked a long-nailed thumb toward the flatbed, which is the word for the back part of a pickup where things are stored. "We used two red herrings to fool you," she said, as the truck's engine roared into life. The children could see, in the back of the truck, the big red herring that had been Lot #48 in the In Auction.

"The Quagmires!" Klaus cried. "Olaf has them trapped inside that statue!" The orphans raced down the steps of the hall, and once again, you may find it more pleasant to put down this book, and close your eyes, and imagine a better ending to this tale than the one that I must write. You may imagine, for instance, that as the Baudelaires reached the truck, they heard the sound of the engine stalling, instead of the tooting of the horn as the hook-handed man drove his bosses away. You may imagine that the children heard the sounds of the Quagmires escaping from the statue of the herring, instead of the word "Toodle-oo!" coming from Esmé's villainous mouth. And you may imagine the sound of police sirens as Count Olaf was caught at last, instead of the weeping of the Baudelaire orphans as the black truck rounded the corner and disappeared from view.

But your imaginings would be ersatz, as all imaginings are. They are as untrue as the ersatz auctioneer who found the Baudelaires at the Squalors' penthouse, and the ersatz elevator outside their front door and the ersatz guardian who pushed them down the deep pit of the elevator shaft. Esmé hid her evil plan behind her reputation as the city's sixth most important financial advisor, and Count Olaf hid his identity behind a monocle and some black boots, and the dark passageway hid its secrets behind a pair of sliding elevator doors, but as much as it pains me to tell you that the Baudelaire orphans stood on the steps of Veblen Hall, weeping with anguish and frustration as Count Olaf rode away with the Quagmire triplets, I cannot hide the unfortunate truths of the Baudelaires' lives behind an ersatz happy ending.

The Baudelaire orphans stood on the steps of Veblen Hall, weeping with anguish and frustration as Count Olaf rode away with the Quagmire triplets, and the sight of Mr. Poe emerging from the award-winning door, with a doily in his hair and a look of panic in his eye, only made them weep harder.

"I'll call the police," Mr. Poe said, "and they'll capture Count Olaf in no time at all," but the Baudelaires knew that this statement was as ersatz as Gunther's improper English. They knew that Olaf was far too clever to be captured by the police, and I'm sorry to say that by the time two detectives found the big black pickup truck, abandoned outside St. Carl's Cathedral with the motor still running, Olaf had already transferred the Quagmires from the red herring to a shiny black instrument case, which he told the bus driver was a tuba he was bringing to his aunt. The three siblings watched Mr. Poe scurry back into Veblen Hall to ask members of the in crowd where he could find a phone booth, and they knew that the banker was not going to be of any help.

"I think Mr. Poe will be a great deal of help," Jerome said, as he walked out of Veblen Hall and sat down on the steps to try to comfort the children. "He's going to call the police, and give them a description of Olaf."

"But Olaf is always in disguise," Violet said miserably, wiping her eyes. "You never know what he'll look like until you see him."

"Well, I'm going to make sure you never see him again," Jerome promised. "Esmé may have left—and I'm not going to argue with her—but I'm still your guardian, and I'm going to take you far, far away from here, so far away that you'll forget all about Count Olaf and the Quagmires and everything else."

"Forget about Olaf?" Klaus asked. "How

can we forget about him? We'll never forget his treachery, no matter where we live."

"And we'll never forget the Quagmires, either," Violet said. "I don't *want* to forget about them. We have to figure out where he's taking our friends, and how to rescue them."

"Tercul!" Sunny said, which meant something along the lines of "And we don't want to forget about everything else, either—like the underground hallway that led to our ruined mansion, and the real meaning of V.F.D.!"

"My sister is right," Klaus said. "We have to track down Olaf and learn all the secrets he's keeping from us."

"We're not going to track down Olaf," Jerome said, shuddering at the thought. "We'll be lucky if he doesn't track us down. As your guardian, I cannot allow you to try to find such a dangerous man. Wouldn't you rather live safely with me?"

"Yes," Violet admitted, "but our friends are in grave danger. We *must* go and rescue them."

"Well, I don't want to argue," Jerome said. "If you've made up your mind, then you've made up your mind. I'll tell Mr. Poe to find you another guardian."

"You mean you won't help us?" Klaus asked.

Jerome sighed, and kissed each Baudelaire on the forehead. "You children are very dear to me," he said, "but I don't have your courage. Your mother always said I wasn't brave enough, and I guess she was right. Good luck, Baudelaires. I think you will need it."

The children watched in amazement as Jerome walked away, not even looking back at the three orphans he was leaving behind. They found their eyes brimming with tears once more as they watched him disappear from sight. They would never see the Squalor penthouse again, or spend another night in their bedrooms, or spend even a moment in their oversized pinstripe suits. Though he was not as dastardly as Esmé or Count Olaf or the hook-handed man, Jerome was still an ersatz guardian, because a real guardian is supposed to provide a home, with a place to sleep and something to wear, and all Jerome had given them in the end was "Good luck." Jerome reached the end of the block and turned left, and the Baudelaires were once again alone in the world.

Violet sighed, and stared down the street in the direction Olaf had escaped. "I hope my inventing skills don't fail me," she said, "because we're going to need more than good luck to rescue the Quagmire triplets."

Klaus sighed, and stared down the street in the direction of the ashy remains of their first home. "I hope my research skills don't fail me," he said, "because we're going to need more than good luck to solve the mystery of the hallway and the Baudelaire mansion."

Sunny sighed, and watched as a lone doily blew down the stairs. "Bite," she said, and she meant that she hoped her teeth wouldn't fail her, because they'd need more than good luck to discover what V.F.D. really stood for.

The Baudelaires looked at one another with faint smiles. They were smiling because they didn't think Violet's inventing skills would fail, any more than Klaus's research skills would fail or Sunny's teeth would fail. But the children also knew that they wouldn't fail each other, as Jerome had failed them and as Mr. Poe was failing them now, as he dialed the wrong number and was talking to a Vietnamese restaurant instead of the police. No matter how many misfortunes had befallen them and no matter how many ersatz things they would encounter in the future, the Baudelaire orphans knew they could rely on each other for the rest of their lives, and this, at least, felt like the one thing in the world that was true.

LEMONY SNICKET'S extended family, if they were

alive, would describe him as a distinguished scholar, an amateur connoisseur, and an outright gentleman. Unfortunately this description has been challenged of late, but Egmont Books continues to support his research and writing on the lives of the Baudelaire orphans.

Lemony Snicket's E-mail to lsnicket@ecb.egmont.com

BRETT HELQUIST was born in Ganado, Arizona, grew up in Orem, Utah, and now lives in New York City. He earned a bachelor's degree in fine arts from Brigham Young University and has been illustrating ever since. His art has appeared in many publications, including *Cricket* magazine and *The New York Times.*

To My Kind Editor,

I am sorry this paper is sopping wet, but I
am writing this from the place where the
Quagmire Triplets were hidden.

The next time you run out of milk,
buy a new carton at Cash Register #19 of
the Not-Very-Supermarket. When you arrive
home, you will find my description of the
Baudelaires' recent experiences in this
dreadful town, entitled THE VILE VILLAGE,
has been tucked into your grocery sack,
along with a burnt-out torch, the tip of a
harpoon, and a chart of the migration paths
of the V.F.D. crows. There is also a copy
of the official portrait of the Council of
Elders, to help Mr. Helquist with his
illustrations.

Remember, you are my last hope that
the tales of the Baudelaire orphans can
finally be told to the general public.

With all due respect,

Lemony Snicket

Lemony Snicket